"I don't know what it is about you, Fiona."

His gaze moved over her features before settling on her eyes. "When I'm with you, I have to touch you. When I'm not with you, I'm thinking about you."

"I feel the same way," she said softly.

He pulled her into his arms and Fiona went willingly. Being with him was worth the price she would eventually have to pay. Reaching up, she cupped his cheeks in her palms and told herself that later on she wouldn't regret this time with him. If memories were all she was going to have, then she wanted a lot of them burned into her mind so that she'd never forget a moment of the time spent with Luke.

He turned his face into her palm and kissed it, sending pearls of heat tumbling through her. Fiona was in deep trouble and she didn't care. What she felt for Luke was so unexpected, such a gift, she couldn't turn away from it.

Dear Reader,

Hi! It's new book time again! And I think you'll really enjoy *Jet Set Confessions*.

In this book, you'll meet Luke Barrett and Fiona Jordan. Luke is the heir to the Barrett Toys and Tech Corporation, but he's frustrated by his grandfather's refusal to take the company into the future. He finally goes out on his own and his grandfather Jamison is desperate to get him back.

Jamison hires Fiona, who has her own company, ICANFIXIT. Fiona can find anything for anyone and now has the job of convincing Luke to rejoin the family business.

Sparks fly between them, but their relationship was founded on the lies Fiona had to tell Luke. When the truth finally comes out, will they be able to get past the mistrust?

I had a great time with these two, and I'm hoping you enjoy them as much as I did!

Visit me on Facebook and let me know what you think!

Until next time, happy reading!

Maureen Child

MAUREEN CHILD

JET SET CONFESSIONS

HARLEQUIN
DESIRE

ISBN-13: 978-1-335-20897-2

Jet Set Confessions

Copyright © 2020 by Maureen Child

This edition published by arrangement with Harlequin Books S.A.

For questions and comments about the quality of this book,
please contact us at CustomerService@Harlequin.com.

Harlequin Enterprises ULC
22 Adelaide St. West, 40th Floor
Toronto, Ontario M5H 4E3, Canada
www.Harlequin.com

Printed in U.S.A.

Maureen Child writes for the Harlequin Desire line and can't imagine a better job. A seven-time finalist for the prestigious Romance Writers of America RITA® Award, Maureen is the author of more than one hundred romance novels. Her books regularly appear on bestseller lists and have won several awards, including a Prism Award, a National Readers' Choice Award, a Colorado Romance Writers Award of Excellence and a Golden Quill Award. She is a native Californian but has recently moved to the mountains of Utah.

Books by Maureen Child

Harlequin Desire

The Tycoon's Secret Child
A Texas-Sized Secret
Little Secrets: His Unexpected Heir
Rich Rancher's Redemption
Billionaire's Bargain
Tempt Me in Vegas
Bombshell for the Boss
Red Hot Rancher
Jet Set Confessions

Visit her Author Profile page at Harlequin.com, or maureenchild.com, for more titles.

You can also find Maureen Child on Facebook, along with other Harlequin Desire authors, at Facebook.com/harlequindesireauthors!

To my mom, Sallye Carberry,
who opened up the world of books to me.
Mom, you taught me to love reading and so much
more. Thank you. I love you.

One

"You've completely lost your mind." Luke Barrett stared across the room at his grandfather. "You said you wanted me to come over to really *talk*. This isn't talking, Pop. This is nuts."

Jamison Barrett stood up from behind his desk, and Luke took just a moment to admire the fact that, at eighty, the old man still stood military-straight. Fit and strong, Jamison was a man to be reckoned with—as he always had been. His steel-gray hair was expertly cut, and he wore a tailored navy-blue pin-striped suit with a power red tie. The look he gave his grandson promised a battle.

"You should know better than to tell an old man

he's crazy," he said. "We're sensitive about that sort of thing."

Luke shook his head. His grandfather had always been stubborn—Luke was used to that. But a few months ago, the old man had dropped a bomb and, clearly, he hadn't changed his mind about it.

"I don't know what else to call this," Luke argued, feeling as frustrated as he had when Pop first brought this up. "When the president of a company suddenly makes a U-turn and wants to cut off its most profitable arm, I think that qualifies as nuts."

Jamison came around the corner of his desk, probably hoping to put this little meeting on a friendlier footing. "I don't have any intention of pulling out of the tech world. I only want to dial it back—"

"Yes," Luke interrupted. "In favor of wooden rocking horses, bicycles and skateboards."

"We're a toy company first," Jamison reminded him. "We have been for more than a hundred damn years."

"And then we *grew* into Barrett Toys and Tech," Luke pointed out.

"Grew in the wrong direction," his grandfather snapped.

"Disagree." Luke blew out a breath and tried to rein in the exasperation nearly choking him. He had always trusted Pop's judgment. But in this, he was willing to fight the older man because, damn it, the path to the future wasn't through the past.

"I've got studies to back me up."

"And I've got profit and loss statements to prove you're wrong."

"Yeah, we're making plenty of money, but is that all we want?"

Luke's jaw dropped. "Since that is sort of the whole point of being in business, I'm going to say *yes*."

Jamison shook his head in clear disappointment. "You used to have a broader vision."

"And you used to listen to me." Irritated, Luke shoved both hands into his slacks pockets and gave a quick glance around his grandfather's office.

It was familiar and warm and pretty much fit the old man to a T. Jamison's desk was a hand-carved mahogany behemoth that dominated the huge room. If there was ever a tidal wave that swept this far inland, Pop could float on that thing for days.

On the cream-colored walls were framed posters of their most popular toys over the years, and family photos dotted the shelves that were also lined with leather-bound books that had actually been read. It was a prestigious Victorian office that seemed at war with the present times.

But then, so was Jamison.

"I don't want to argue with you about this again, Pop," Luke said, trying to keep the impatience he was feeling out of his tone.

He owed this proud old man everything. Jamison and his wife, Loretta, had raised Luke and his cousin Cole after the boys' parents were killed in a small plane crash. Luke had been ten and Cole twelve when they went to live with their grandparents as broken, grief-stricken kids. But Jamison and Loretta had picked up the pieces in spite of their own grief at losing both of their sons and daughters-in-law in one horrific accident. They had given their grandsons love and protection and the feeling that their world hadn't ended.

Luke and Cole had grown up working at Barrett Toys, knowing that one day they would be in charge. The company was more than a hundred years old and had always stayed current by leaping into the future—taking chances. When Luke was in college and convinced his grandfather that tech toys were going to be the next big thing, Jamison hadn't hesitated.

He'd gathered up the finest tech designers he could find, and the Barrett toy company got even bigger, even more successful. Now they were on the cutting edge. Counted as one of the biggest toy and tech companies in the world. For the last few years, Luke had been running the tech division, and Cole worked on the more traditional outlet.

Okay yes, Cole wasn't happy that Luke was the heir apparent, especially since he was two years older than Luke, but the cousins had worked that out. Mostly.

Now, though, none of them knew where they stood. All because Jamison Barrett had gotten a bug up his—

"I'm not talking about an argument, Luke," Jamison said, clearly irritated. "I'm talking about what I see every time I walk out of this office. Hell, Luke, if you weren't glued to your phone like the rest of humanity, you'd see it, too."

As irritated as his grandfather, Luke bit back his temper. He'd heard this argument over and over during the last couple of months. "Not this again."

"Yes, *this*. This is about the kids, Luke. As attached to their phones and screens and tablets and games as you are to your email." Jamison threw both hands high. "Used to be, children were running amok outside with their friends, getting into trouble, climbing trees, swimming." He glared at Luke. "Hell, you and Cole were in constant motion when you were kids. Making you stay inside and read was looked at like torture!"

All true, he thought, but he only said, "Times change."

Jamison scowled. "Not always for the better. Kids today, all their friends are online, and they wear headsets so they can talk to each other without actually having to see each other. Instead of getting outside, they build 'virtual' tree houses. They have carefully written adventures via game boxes."

"Hell, most kids probably don't even know *how* to ride a bike anymore."

Luke shook his head. "Bikes aren't going to teach them how to navigate what's becoming a completely digital world."

"Right. A digital world." Jamison nodded sharply. "Who's going to fix your cars, or air conditioners, or the damn toilet when it breaks? You going to pee digitally, too? It's going to get mighty hot in your house if you're only using virtual air-conditioning."

"This is ridiculous," Luke muttered, amazed that he had allowed himself to get sucked into Jamison's fixation. He had to wonder where his visionary grandfather had gone. Did this happen to *all* old people? Did they all start slipping into a hole and then pulling the hole in after them?

"Pop, you're making the same kind of complaint every generation makes about the newer one. You've never been the kind of man to look backward. You've always been more interested in the future than the past. This isn't like you."

"Times change." Jamison tossed Luke's words back at him. "And I *am* talking about the future," the older man argued. "There are all kinds of studies out now about what staring at screens are doing to kids' minds. That's why I wanted you to come in. I want you to see them. Read them. Open your damn mind long enough to admit that *maybe* I've got a point."

With that, Jamison turned to his desk and started riffling through the papers and files stacked there. Muttering beneath his breath, he checked everywhere, then checked again.

"I had it right here," he muttered. "Had Donna print it all out this morning." Facing Luke again, he said, "I can't find it right now and damned if I can figure out why—"

Luke frowned. "Doesn't matter."

"That's where you're wrong. Blast it, Luke, I don't want to be part of ruining a generation of children."

"Ruining?" Astonished, Luke stared at him. *"*We're giving kids a step up, helping them learn to read—"

"Their parents could do that by reading to them at night."

"Toddlers learn colors and puzzle solving with our games."

"They can do that with a box of crayons."

"God, you're a hardhead."

"First, I'm losing my mind, and now I'm just old and stubborn, is that it?" Jamison's eyes flashed. "Well, I can tell you I'm sharper than you are if you can't see the truth in what I'm telling you."

Luke shoved both hands through his hair. Maybe he hadn't really come to his grandfather's office. Maybe he was home in bed having a nightmare. Or maybe he'd taken a sharp left turn on the way here and had somehow ended up in hell.

His grandfather had always been on the current edge of everything. This about-face had really thrown Luke. He looked at Jamison's attitude now as not trusting Luke to take the helm of the company. As if he'd been indulging Luke and, now, was pulling the rug out from under him.

He took a deep breath, reminded himself that he

loved the old man currently driving him bat-crap crazy and said, "You know what? We're just not going to agree on this, Pop. We need to stop hammering at each other over it. It's better if both of us just keep doing what we're doing."

Or at least what they had been doing the last couple of months. When Jamison first told Luke about his idea to scale back the tech division, Luke had argued until his head throbbed. He'd presented his case against the idea, which Pop had quickly dismissed. It hadn't been the first time they'd locked horns and fought it out, but somehow that argument had felt more…final than any of the others. When it was over, Luke had taken a stand and left the company to go out on his own. If nothing else, he was going to prove to his grandfather that he had faith in his own plans. Prove that tech toys really were the wave of the future.

"That's it? We just part ways? That's your final word on this?"

He met his grandfather's dark green eyes. It felt like the chasm between them was getting wider by the second. For now, Luke was going to concentrate on building his own tech toy company, Go Zone. "It is, Pop. The past can't build the future."

"You can't have a future *without* a past," Jamison pointed out.

"And the carousel keeps turning," Luke muttered. "Every time we talk about this, we say the same things, and neither one of us is convinced. We're on opposite sides of this, Pop. And there is no bridge. For me, it's better if I stay out on my own."

"Your grandmother cried last night. Over all of this."

Instantly, a sharp pang of guilt stabbed Luke but, then, he thought about it. Loretta Barrett was as tough as they came. His grandfather was sneaky enough to try to use his wife to win the argument. "No, she didn't."

Jamison scowled. "No, she didn't," he admitted. "She yelled some. But she could have cried. Probably will."

Luke blew out a breath and shook his head. "You're impossible."

"I'm doing what I have to do. You belong *here*, Luke, not running your own place."

And honestly, Luke had thought that Barrett Toys *was* his place. But things had changed with Pop's change of heart. With what felt to Luke as his lack of faith. His grandfather had always pushed him, believed in him. Trusted him. This felt like a betrayal, plain and simple. Luke's new company was small, but he had some great designers, just out of college, filled with ideas that would shake up the toy tech business. Luke was hoping to get manufacturing up and pumping out his new line by the end of the year.

This had all started because he'd been frustrated with his grandfather—but now, Luke was committed to making this work. Jamison might be willing to turn his back on progress, but Luke was greeting it with open arms.

"This is the *Barrett* toy company," Jamison reminded him. "A Barrett has been in charge since the beginning. Family, Luke. That's what's important."

That's what made all of this so much harder.

"We're still family, Pop," he reminded the older man—and himself at the same time. "And remember, you've got Cole here to run the business if you ever decide to retire."

"Cole's not you," Jamison said flatly. "I love the boy, but he hasn't got the head for the business that you do."

"He'll come around," Luke said, though he didn't really believe it. Hell, it's why Luke had been Jamison's choice to run the company in the first place. Cole just wasn't interested in the day-to-day of running a business. He liked being in charge. Liked the money. But he was a delegator, not a worker.

"You always were a stubborn one," Jamison muttered.

"Wonder where I got that," Luke said wryly.

"Touché." Nodding, his grandfather said, "Fine. You do what you have to do, so will I."

Luke hated having this simmering tension between him and his grandfather. Jamison Barrett was the rock in Luke's life. The old man had taught him how to fish, how to throw a fastball and how to tie a bow tie. He'd taught Luke everything about running a business and how to treat employees. He'd been there. Always. And now, Luke felt like he was abandoning him. But damned if he could think of a way to end it so that both of them came out winning.

"Give my love to Gran."

He left before his grandfather could say anything else, closing the office door behind him. The company headquarters was in Foothill Ranch, California, and most of the windows looked out over palm trees, more buildings and parking lots. Still, there was a greenbelt nearby and enough sunlight pouring through the lightly tinted windows to make the whole place bright.

Jamison's secretary, Donna, looked up from her computer screen. She was comfortably in her fifties and had been with Jamison for thirty years. "See you, Luke."

"Yeah," he answered, giving his grandfather's door one last look. He didn't like leaving the old man like this, but what choice did he have?

Still frowning to himself, he asked, "Is Cole here?"

"Yep." Donna nodded toward a bank of offices across the room.

"Thanks." Luke headed over to see his cousin. He gave a brisk knock, then opened the door and stuck his head in. "How's it going?"

"Hey." Cole looked up and smiled. Even in a suit, he looked like a typical California surfer. Tanned, fit, with sun-streaked blond hair and blue eyes, Cole Barrett was the charmer in the company. He did lunches with prospective clients and took meetings with manufacturers because he could usually smooth-talk people into just about anything. "You here to see Pop?"

"Just left him." Luke braced one shoulder on the doorjamb and idly noted how different Cole's office was from their grandfather's. Smaller, of course, but that was to be expected. It was more than that, though. Cole's desk was steel and glass, his desk chair black leather minimalist. Shelves were lined with some of the toys their company had produced over the years, but the walls were dotted with professionally done photos of his wife, Susan, and their toddler son, Oliver—skiing in Switzerland, visiting the Pyramids and aboard the family yacht. Cole had always been more interested in playing than in the work required to make the money to do the playing.

Luke dismissed it all and met his cousin's eyes. "Wanted to warn you that he's still not happy about me leaving."

Cole leaned back in his desk chair and steepled his fingers. "No surprise there. You were the golden boy, destined to run Barrett Toys..."

Bitterness colored Cole's tone, but Luke was used to that. "That's changed."

"Only because you left." His cousin shook his head. "Pop is still determined to bring you back into the fold."

Pushing away from the wall, Luke straightened

up. "Not going to happen. I've got my own company now."

Cole swung his chair lazily back and forth. "It's not Barrett, though, is it?"

No, it wasn't. A start-up company was fun. Challenging, even. But it wasn't like running Barrett's. He'd poured a lot of work and heart into the family business. But feeling as he did now, that his grandfather didn't trust him, how could he run Barrett's with any sort of confidence? "It will be," he said, with determination. "Someday."

"Right. Anyway." Cole stood up, slipped his suit jacket on and buttoned it. "I've got a lunch meeting."

"Fine. Just…" He thought about Pop, rooting around for those papers and looking confused about why he couldn't find them. "Keep me posted on Pop, will you?"

"Why?"

Luke shrugged. "He's getting old."

"Not to hear him tell it," Cole said with a short scrape of a laugh.

"Yeah, I know that." Luke nodded and told himself he'd done what he'd gone there to do—try one more time to get through to his grandfather. Make him see reason. Now it was time to move the hell on. "All right, then. I've got a plane to catch. So, say hello to Susan and Oliver for me."

"I will."

When he walked out, Luke didn't look back.

* * *

Jamison stood at his open office door and watched his grandson. An all-too-familiar stir of frustration had him falling back into the old habit of jingling the coins in his pockets.

"You're jingling."

He stopped instantly and shot a look at his assistant.

"Didn't work, did it?" she asked.

"No one likes hearing 'I told you so,' Donna."

She shrugged. "I didn't say it."

"You were thinking it."

"If you're such a good mind reader," the woman countered, "you should have known telling him that Loretta cried was a mistake."

She had a point. No one who knew his wife would believe she'd given in to a bout of tears.

"Fine," he grudgingly admitted. "You were right. Happy?"

"I'm not unhappy. It's always good to be right."

He scowled at the woman currently ignoring him as she busily typed up some damn thing or other. Donna had been with him for thirty years and never let him forget it.

Shaking his head, Jamison shifted his gaze back to Luke as he walked across the room, stopping to chat with people on his way to the elevator. He was leaving, and Jamison didn't have a clue how to get him back. So it seemed it was time for the big guns.

"The woman you told me about. You still think she can help?"

Donna stopped typing and looked up at him. "Apparently, she's pretty amazing, so maybe."

Jamison nodded. He wanted his grandson back in the company, damn it. How the hell could he ever retire if Luke wasn't there to take over for him? Cole was good at his specified job, but he didn't have it in him to keep growing Barrett Toys. Jamison needed Luke.

"Well, I tried the easy way," he murmured. "Now it's time to put on the pressure."

"Boss…if Luke finds out, this could all go bad in a huge way."

He dismissed her warning with an idle wave of a hand. "Then we'll have to make sure he doesn't find out, won't we? Make the call, Donna. I'll be waiting in my office."

"I've got a bad feeling about this," she said as she picked up the phone and started dialing.

Jamison turned to his office, but paused long enough to ask, "Where are those statistics I asked you to print out for me this morning?"

Frowning, she looked at him. "I put them on your desk first thing."

"You didn't move them?"

"Why would I do that?"

"Right, right." He nodded and tried to remember what he'd done with the damn things. Then something else occurred to him. "Okay, make the call.

And Donna, there's no reason to tell Loretta any of this."

She rolled her eyes.

"I saw that."

"Wasn't hiding it," she countered.

"I am your boss, you know."

"Don't let it go to your head," Donna advised.

The next afternoon, Fiona Jordan walked into the restaurant at the Gables, a five-star hotel in San Francisco. The best part about owning her own business? She just never knew what would happen from day to day. Yesterday, she'd been working out of her duplex in Long Beach, California, and today, she was in a gorgeous hotel in San Francisco.

Smiling to herself, she took a breath and scanned the busy room.

White-cloth-draped tables and booths were crowded, and the hum of conversation, heavy silverware clinking against plates and the piped-in violin music streaming from discreetly hidden speakers created an atmosphere of luxury. There were windows all along one wall that afforded a spectacular view of the Bay, where the afternoon sun was busily painting a bright golden trail across the surface of the water.

But at the moment, the view wasn't her priority, Fiona thought as she did a more detailed scan of the room. She was here to find one particular person.

When she found him, her heart gave a quick, hard

jolt, and a buzz of something hot and potentially dangerous zipped through her.

Luke Barrett. He had sun-streaked, light brown hair that was just long enough to curl over the collar of his dark blue suit jacket. Gaze focused on the phone he held, he seemed oblivious to the people surrounding him and completely content to be alone.

Fiona didn't really understand that. She liked people. Talking to them, hearing their stories—everyone had a story—and discovering what she liked about them. But she'd already been warned that Luke was so wrapped up in his work, he barely noticed the people around him.

So, she told herself, she'd simply have to be unforgettable.

Luke sat alone at a window table, but he paid no attention to the view. Fiona, on the other hand, was enjoying her view of him a little too much. Even in profile, he was more gorgeous than the picture she'd been given.

That buzz of something interesting shot straight through her again, and she took a moment to enjoy it. It had been a long time since a man had elicited that sort of reaction from her. Heck, she couldn't even remember the last time she'd felt a zing of interest.

Her gaze went back to his just-a-little-long hair and realized that it was an intriguing choice for a corporate type. Maybe Luke Barrett was going to be much more than she'd expected. But there was still the whole wrapped-up-in-his-phone thing to get past.

Fiona watched as a beautiful woman strolled by Luke's table, giving him a smile that most men would have drooled over—he didn't notice.

"Hmm." Realizing that meeting Luke Barrett might call for a little extra punch, Fiona turned toward the long sinuous sweep of the bar. She ordered a glass of chardonnay, gave the bartender a big tip and a smile, took a deep breath, and studied her target.

Then Fiona tossed her long, dark brown hair over her shoulder and started for his table. The short hem of her flirty black skirt swirled around her thighs and her mile-high black heels tapped cheerfully against the glossy floor. Her dark green long-sleeved blouse had a deeply scooped neckline, and gold hoops dangled from her earlobes.

She looked great, even if she was saying it herself, and it was a shame to ruin the outfit, but desperate times…

A waiter passed in front of her; Fiona deliberately stumbled, took a couple of halting steps, and with a slight shriek, threw herself and a full glass of very nice wine into Luke Barrett's lap.

Two

Luke's first instinct was to grab hold of the woman who had dropped into his lap from out of nowhere. She smiled up at him, and he felt a punch of desire slam into his chest. When she squirmed on his lap, he felt that punch a lot lower.

"What the hell?" He looked into a pair of chocolate-brown eyes and realized she was laughing.

"Sorry, sorry!" She squirmed again, and he instantly held her still. "I guess I stumbled on something. Thank God you were here, or I'd have fallen onto something a lot harder."

He didn't know about that. He felt pretty damn hard at the moment. And wet. He felt wet, as the wine she'd been carrying now seeped into his shirt and pants. Even as he thought it, she half turned around, grabbed a cloth napkin and dabbed at the wine splashed across her blouse, then started in on his shirt. If she tried to dry his pants, he was a dead man.

"What'd you trip on?" He glanced down at the floor and saw nothing.

"I don't know," she admitted, then shrugged helplessly. "Sometimes I trip on air."

"Good to know."

She tipped her head to one side and long, dark brown hair slid across her shoulders. "Are you going to let me up?"

It wasn't his first thought. "Are you going to fall again?"

"Well, I'm not sure," she admitted with a grin. "Anything's possible."

"Then maybe it's safer if you stay where you are," Luke mused, still caught by the smile in those brown eyes of hers.

She started her fruitless dabbing at his shirt again. Not unlike trying to soak up the ocean with a sponge.

"Yeah," he said, taking the napkin from her. "Never mind."

"Well, I do feel badly about this," she said.

"Me, too."

"In all fairness, though," she pointed out, "I got plenty of the wine on my shirt, as well."

"And that should make me happy?"

She shrugged and her dark green off-the-shoulder shirt dipped a bit.

Instantly, his gaze dropped to the full swell of her breasts and he wondered if he'd get more of a look if she shrugged again. When he lifted his gaze to hers, he saw a knowing smile.

A waiter hustled up to them with several napkins, then just stood there as if unsure what his next move should be. Luke could sympathize.

Finally, the waiter asked, "Are you all right, miss?"

"Oh, I'm fine."

She was fine. He was being tortured but, apparently, no one cared about that.

"I'm so sorry, Mr. Barrett. Is there anything I can do?"

"No," he said grimly. "I think it's all been done."

"Well, there is one thing…" His mystery lap dancer spoke up. "My wine's gone." She held up the empty glass like it was a visual aid.

"And I know where it went," Luke muttered.

The waiter looked from Luke to the woman and back again. Still unsure. Still worried. Luke was used to that. He was rich. His family was famous. Most people got nervous around him. And he hated that. So he forced a smile and said, "Would you get the lady another glass of wine, Michael?"

"Certainly. What were you drinking, miss?"

"Chardonnay, thanks. The house wine's fine."

Luke frowned and shook his head. "I think we can do better than that, can't we, Michael?"

The waiter grinned. "Yes, sir."

When the man left, Luke looked into those chocolate eyes again. "So, since you're sitting on my lap, I think it's only right I know your name."

"Oh, I'm Fiona. Fiona Jordan." She held out a hand to him.

He glanced at it and smirked. "I think we've already moved past a handshake, don't you?"

"I think we have," she said. "And since your lap is being so welcoming, maybe I could know your name? Last name Barrett, according to the waiter. First name?"

"Luke."

She tipped her head to one side and studied him for a long second or two. "I like it. Short. Strong. Sounds like a romance novel hero."

This had to be the strangest conversation he'd ever had.

Nodding, he confessed, "You found my secret. By day, I'm a tech-toy developer. But at night, I'm a pirate or a lord or a Highlander."

She gave him a wide grin, and that punch of desire hit him harder. "How is it you know so much about romance novels?"

"My grandmother goes through a dozen every week. I grew up seeing books with half-dressed men and women on the covers scattered around the house."

"A well-rounded childhood, then."

Luke thought about that and had to say, she was right. In spite of losing his parents when he was just a child, Luke's grandparents had saved him. They'd given him normalcy again. Made sure that though his world had been rocked, it hadn't been completely destroyed.

His lips quirked. "I always thought so."

"I envy you," she said simply, and before he could comment, the waiter was back.

Michael hurried up, carrying a glass of wine for Fiona and a refill of Luke's scotch. He set both glasses on the table and said, "On the house, Mr. Barrett. And again, we're very sorry about—"

"You don't have to apologize, Michael," Fiona told him. "I'm the clumsy one."

The man winced. "Oh, I wouldn't say clumsy…"

"That's because you don't smell like chardonnay," Luke put in wryly.

Michael nodded again before he scurried away.

"I think you scared him," Fiona said as she watched the man rush back to the bar.

"I think you're the one who scared him. Pretty women can have that effect on a man," Luke countered.

She turned back and literally beamed at him. "But not you?"

"I'm immune."

"Good to know," she said, smiling. "Does that mean I should give up or try even harder to be scary?"

"Oh, definitely keep trying." Luke grinned. Hell, he liked a woman this sure of herself. Well, to be honest, he just liked women. But a strong, gorgeous one with a sense of humor was right at the top of the list. And this one was more intriguing than most. It had been a long time since a woman had made this kind of impact on him. He laughed to himself at that thought, because she had landed on him with both physical and emotional impacts.

He took a quick look at the whole package. Long, dark brown hair, those chocolate eyes, a wide mouth, now curved in a smile, and a body that filled his mind with all kinds of interesting images. That green shirt looked great on her, and the full black skirt was short enough to showcase some great legs. The mile-high black heels just put the finishing touches on the whole picture. Oh yeah, she could be dangerous.

Even to a man who had no intention of getting into a "relationship," Luke loved women, and the occasional date or one-night stand was great. But he didn't have the time or the patience to devote himself to two passions right now. All of his focus had to be on his budding company. So meeting a woman like this one could be problematic.

"So…" Fiona spoke again, and Luke told himself to listen up. "Now that we're so comfy with each other, what brings you to San Francisco?"

"I don't know if *comfy* is the right word," Luke said wryly, shifting position a bit.

She reached for her wine, but Luke was faster. He handed her the glass. He wasn't going to risk another wine bath.

"What's the matter?" she asked. "Don't you trust me?"

"Since my shirt is still wet from your last glass of wine, I'm going to say no."

She laughed. "Well, that's honest, anyway. I like honest. But I have to say, I think it's time I moved to a chair."

He reached for his scotch and took a sip. The aged whiskey sent a slow burn through his body that couldn't even compare to the current blaze centered in his lap. "Yeah, maybe you should." He knew everyone in the restaurant had to be watching them, and Luke didn't give a flying damn. Fiona Jordan had broken up his afternoon and brightened a long, boring day, and he was going to enjoy it. In fact, he hadn't felt this…light since the day before with his grandfather.

Something about her made him forget the things plaguing him and, for that, he was grateful. Just before she'd dropped into his lap, he'd been going over and over again that conversation with Pop. Wondering if he could have handled things better. Hating that the two of them were at such odds.

But this woman with the brilliant smile and the gorgeous legs had changed that—for however long the feeling lasted.

She hopped up, and Luke muffled a groan as she took a seat across the table from him.

He had to admit he was breathing easier, even when she took a sip of her wine, then ran the tip of her tongue across her top lip to catch a stray drop. His gaze locked on that movement and yet one more sharp jab of heat stabbed him. He couldn't remember the last time a woman had attracted him so completely. And while warning bells were going off in the back of his mind, Luke ignored them all.

She took another sip of her wine, met his gaze across the table and asked, "So, what should we talk about?"

His eyebrows arched. "You want to have a conversation now?"

She shrugged. "You want to sit here in silence?"

She had a point. "Fine. Let's talk."

"Great." She took a sip of wine. "You start."

All he could really think about was what she was doing to him. Hard to come up with a conversational starter beyond *Let's go upstairs to my room.* "No. You start."

"Okay." She shrugged, and the bodice of her blouse dipped again. "What're you doing at the hotel?"

"At the moment, trying to keep my mind busy."

She grinned. "Let me rephrase. Are you from San Francisco?"

"No," he said. "I'm from Orange County. Newport Beach, specifically."

She grinned. "We're practically neighbors, then. I live in Long Beach. So, why are you here?"

"Business," Luke told her. "I'm here for the tech conference." Though he hadn't been enjoying it until she had dropped onto his lap. With all the thoughts racing through his mind—his grandfather, Barrett's, his own new company, he'd been silently stewing. She'd interrupted all of that.

"Ah." She nodded and gave a quick glance around the restaurant. "A conference. That explains all of the badges, not to mention the fact that everyone I see has their nose glued to a phone or computer."

He took a look, too, and had to admit that almost everyone in the dining area was reading a phone or scrolling on a tablet. Even at a table with six people sitting around it, all of them were busy with their own phones. He frowned a little, then shrugged it off. This conference was, as he'd said, for business.

"Guilty," he said, turning his gaze back to her.

"So if you're here for the conference, you're in the tech business, right?"

"I am." One of the reasons he came to these conferences was that here, he was surrounded by other forward-thinking people like him. People who understood that the future was in binary. "My company makes tech toys."

"Tech toys?" She tipped her head to one side. "What kind?"

She actually seemed interested, and there was nothing he liked more than to talk about the latest in tech toys. If Pop hadn't changed his mind, Luke would be even more eager to talk about them. He'd imagined steering Barrett's into the future. Drawing on their already trusted name in toys to introduce kids to the what was to come. Still, his new company would do all of that. It would just take longer to take off. To get recognition. Luke took the conversational thread and ran with it. "All kinds. From tablets that are user-friendly for toddlers, to gaming boards, video games and miniature robots and drones." He took a sip of his scotch. "We've got a full line of tech toys for every age."

She laughed again and the sound of it was like champagne bubbles.

"I barely understand my computer *now*. I can't imagine a toddler on one."

"You'd be surprised. Our test groups do very well at color and spatial relations and problem solving on the screen." He hadn't been able to convince his grandfather of that, of course. Because Jamison was concerned about pumping too much information into growing minds. But Luke believed that a young, open mind was far more likely to absorb information. And how was that a bad thing?

"There have been dozens of studies to prove that in children as young as one, the brain is like a sponge, soaking up information far faster than it will in the future."

She shook her head. "My best friend has a toddler whose main focus is eating the dog's kibble."

He laughed. "Maybe he needs a tablet."

"Maybe," she allowed. "Still, I'm amazed at the idea of babies on computers. But maybe I need a toddler to walk me through running my Word program."

Luke smiled at her.

"So, I guess 'tech toys' means you don't make bikes and dolls and things?"

His last encounter with his grandfather was still

fresh in his mind, so his response was a little sharper than it should have been when he said, "No. The future isn't made up of dolls and bikes and Frisbees. It's in electronics."

She held up both hands in mock surrender. "Whoa. Okay. You convinced me. I give up."

Luke took a breath and blew it out again, reaching for calm. Wasn't her fault that his grandfather was suddenly retreating into the past. "Yeah, sorry. Sore spot. My grandfather and I have been going around and around about this."

"That has to be hard, disagreeing with family." She sipped at her wine. "Why are you?"

No way was he getting into all of that right now. "Long story."

She nodded as if she understood he simply didn't want to talk about it. But then she asked, "All right. But I'm still not convinced that tablets for toddlers are a good idea. Even tiny sponges need a teddy bear."

He smiled again, glad she'd dropped it. Back on safe ground, ground he knew like the back of his hand, he said, "There are plenty of companies that sell stuffed animals or dolls or whatever else you think a kid should have. But the future for kids today will be in technology, so shouldn't they get a jump as young as possible?"

She still looked unconvinced. "But toddlers?"

"Sure. If we can get children as young as two involved with electronics, their brains will develop faster, and they'll be more inclined toward the sciences. That's a win. For all of us."

"The sciences." She smiled. "Like making mud pies in the backyard?"

"You're a hard sell, aren't you?" He stared into her eyes and liked the feeling of being pulled in. A damn shame, he thought, that he could have a real conversation about what was important to him with a stranger—but his own grandfather wouldn't listen.

"I'm just saying that being comfortable with tech at a young age will make them more accepting of it later." As an example, he said, "We use colors and shapes and sound to get their interest." He was warming to the theme, as he always did. "They learn without realizing they're learning. Studies prove out that children who are challenged rise to the occasion more often than not."

"But aren't there just as many studies saying that it's not good to introduce small kids to tech too early?"

"You sound like my grandfather," he said.

"Thank you?" She laughed a little. "Not trying to argue, I just think that there are two sides to this and maybe your grandfather has a point."

Luke grumbled under his breath. It wasn't easy arguing for the future when everyone wanted to cling to the past. "My grandfather won't even listen to the arguments on this, so it's pointless to try any further."

"Have you listened to his side?"

Luke took another sip of his scotch and studied

her. He was trying to decide if he should keep talking or change the subject. She took care of that for him.

"It sounds interesting," she said. "And a little scary."

Frowning, he sipped at his scotch. Now that too sounded like his grandfather's argument. "Why?"

"Because I like watching little kids pick dandelions or splash in mud puddles." She shrugged and took another sip of her wine. "They should be outside, running and playing. Seeing them staring at a screen instead just seems wrong. I mean, once you grow up, you're always on a computer. Why start before you have to?"

"Because it's fun?"

"If you say so." She shook her head and her gorgeous hair slid back and forth across her shoulders. "I have a love-hate relationship with my computer."

"You like email and the internet, right?"

"Sure. But I hate a full inbox. Drives me crazy."

"A full inbox means your business is doing well."

"Except for the spam."

He brushed that off. "Downside to everything."

He wondered why he wasn't as irritated with Fiona as he became with his grandfather when they had pretty much this same conversation. His phone buzzed, and Luke glanced at the screen before shifting it to voice mail. He wasn't in the position or in the mood to take a call from his grandfather.

"You don't have to get that?" she asked.

"Absolutely not."

"Okay, then." She set her wine down on the table.

His gaze dropped to her fingers sliding up and down the faceted stem of the glass.

Instantly, his body went rock hard again.

"So," he said abruptly, "since I'm pretty much trapped in this chair for a while, why don't you stay and have a late lunch with me."

She chewed at her bottom lip and with every tug of her teeth, Luke felt an answering tug inside him.

Finally, Fiona said, "I suppose that's fair, since I'm the reason you're trapped in that chair for a while."

"You are." He hadn't planned on company, but what the hell? Beautiful woman or doing email alone? Not really a contest.

"Okay, then." She crossed those great legs and swung her right foot lazily. Propping her elbows on the table, she leaned in and smiled. "Feeling better yet?"

He should have been. But he was still hard, and he missed the feel of her lush body plopped on top of his. That probably made him a masochist.

"Strangely enough, no."

A slow, wide smile curved her mouth. "Just what I was thinking."

Heat pulsed inside him and fed the flames keeping his dick at full alert. Hell, at this rate, he was going to have to hire someone to walk in front of him just to get out of the damn restaurant.

She picked up her wine, took a sip, then flicked out her tongue again to sweep away another stray drop from her top lip. Fire burning even hotter now, he thought.

"You're doing that on purpose, aren't you?"

Her mouth curved into a smile. "Is it working?"

"Too damn well," he admitted, and her smile spread further.

When the waiter brought menus, she flipped through hers until she got to the burgers.

Surprised, he asked, "A woman who's *not* going for a salad?"

She lifted her gaze to his and shook her head. "That's completely sexist. You know that, right?"

He shrugged the comment off. "Every woman I've ever taken to dinner ordered some kind of salad."

"Clearly, you're dating the wrong women." She closed the menu and folded her hands on top of it. "I'm an unapologetic carnivore. Burgers. Steaks. Love them all."

Nodding, Luke just looked at her, enjoying the view. "Good to know. And today? Burger or steak?"

"The San Francisco burger, hold the avocado."

"You don't like avocado?"

"Ew." Her features screwed up. "No."

"I don't know if I can have lunch with you after all," Luke said.

Her eyes sparkled. "So you have standards?"

"Doesn't everyone?"

"And avocado is one of them?"

"We live in California. Guacamole is a way of life here," Luke said.

"Not my life," she assured him. "I love Mexican

food, but avocados are a deal breaker. It's a texture thing. They're too slimy."

"Have you tasted one?"

"God, no. I have standards, too." She grinned and Luke's insides stirred again.

The waiter came back, Luke gave him their order, then leaned back with his scotch to study the woman who had become the focus of his attention. Her bare shoulders made him think about sliding that pretty green shirt down her arms so he could feast on her breasts. His dick hardened even further, though he wouldn't have thought that possible, and his hands itched to touch her.

Fiona shifted beneath his steady stare and fought down the rise of heat threatening to engulf her. She seriously had not been prepared for the rush of something…*tantalizing* that she'd felt the moment she saw Luke Barrett. But how could she have been? All she'd had was his picture and a brief description of where she was most likely to find him.

No one had said his eyes were the color of the ocean on a summer day. Or that he was tall and muscular beneath that well-cut suit or that his hair was too long and sun-streaked. And there was no way she'd expected the deep timbre of his voice to rumble along her spine.

Mostly, though, she hadn't been prepared for the hot, throbbing ache that had settled between her thighs from sitting on his lap and feeling the hard press of him against her. Just remembering made her squirm a bit in her seat, as if to rekindle the sensation.

But she wasn't here to "kindle" anything. She was here because she'd given her word to someone. Taken a job. Made a promise. And Fiona always kept her promises.

She smiled because Luke looked at her as if he were trying to read her mind, and she was grateful he couldn't. Liking him was okay, liking him too much could jeopardize her job and that had to come first. She'd been offered a twenty-thousand dollar bonus if she succeeded. And she needed that money.

With an actual savings account, she could buy a car that didn't run on hopes and dreams and invest in her own business to help it grow.

"What are you thinking?" His question shattered the thoughts he was asking about.

Fiona had to scramble. "Just wondering how a man gets into tech toys," she said, and silently congratulated herself on coming up with that so quickly.

He took a sip of his scotch and set the heavy glass tumbler down again. "Started in the family business." He shrugged. "Recently I went out on my own."

"Really. Why?"

He gave her a suspicious look. "Why do you care?"

"I don't," she lied. "Just curious. Is this about your disagreement with your grandfather?"

"And why should I feed a stranger's curiosity?"

"Oh," Fiona said with a slow smile, "after what

we've already shared, I don't think we're strangers anymore."

He laughed shortly and inclined his head. "Point taken. Okay, you're right. My grandfather and I couldn't see eye to eye."

"Isn't there a compromise in there somewhere?"

"Not with Pop. He prefers the past, and I want the future."

Basically what she already knew. "Sounds dire."

"No." One firm shake of his head. "Just business."

"Even with family?"

"Family adds another layer, but it still boils down to business." Frowning, he said, "My grandfather and I had a plan. He changed his mind, so I'm going ahead with the plan on my own. Simple."

"Is it? Simple, I mean."

"It will be," he said, nodding to himself.

He clammed up fast after that, and Fiona once again silently warned herself to go slowly. Carefully. His eyes were closed off, shuttered as if he'd erected a privacy wall around his thoughts. And she had a feeling that she'd never get past that wall by using a battering ram. He was clearly a private person, so that would make getting him to open up to her more difficult. And despite what he'd just said, she knew there was nothing simple about his situation.

Yet she had to wonder how he could shut out a grandfather who loved him. Fiona didn't have family. She had friends. Lots of friends, because she'd set out to *create* a family. She couldn't imagine turning her back on a grandfather who loved her.

Wistfully, she wondered briefly what that might be like and wondered why Luke couldn't see how lucky he was to have the very family he was at odds with.

Their lunch arrived then and they both went quiet as the waiter set the plates in front of them, then filled water goblets.

Luke had ordered the same burger she had, but *with* avocado. "Sure you don't want to try it?"

She held out one hand in a "stop" gesture. "Way sure."

"You could look at this as an opportunity to expand your horizons."

She laughed. "With an avocado?"

"It's a start." His eyes flashed and a new jolt of heat swept through Fiona.

"I think we could find a better place to start expanding those horizons," she said quietly. "Don't you?"

He looked at her for a long moment, the heat in his eyes searing every inch of her skin. "I can work with that."

Three

Back in Laguna Beach, Jamison walked into his house and strode directly into the living room. As always, he was struck at the silence in the big house. When Cole and Luke were young, there was laughter, shouting, the dogs barking and dozens of the kids' friends running in and out. Now that it was just him and his wife, Loretta, sometimes the quiet became overpowering.

The muffled voices from the television pulled him into the big room. Loretta was curled up in the corner of a couch, watching a flat-screen TV hanging on the wall above a fireplace, where gas flames danced over faux logs. She glanced at him and smiled, and Jamison felt that hard punch of love that always left him feeling off-balance.

From the first moment they'd met, almost sixty years ago now, Jamison thought with a jolt, he'd loved Loretta. She was the best thing that had ever happened to him and, as the years passed, that only became clearer to him.

Young people might think love was only for them, but Jamison was here to testify that flames didn't burn out, they only got warmer, steadier, and the love that fanned them, richer.

"Hi, hon," she said. "How was your day?"

"Frustrating," he admitted with a scowl and gave a quick look around the room. Usually, he walked in here and felt better. Loretta had decorated the place in soothing tones of blue and greens that always reminded Jamison of the sea. Overstuffed couches and chairs, gleaming oak tables, and a stained-glass window on one wall that tossed colored patches of light onto the hardwood floor. It was a room made for relaxation but, today, he knew it wasn't going to help him.

Jamison walked to the wet bar across the room, poured himself a scotch and took the first gulp like it was medicine.

"Tell me what happened." Loretta hit the mute button and instantly, silence dropped onto the room.

"Still thinking about another fruitless argument with Luke yesterday."

"Oh, Jamie, for God's sake, let it go."

He stared at her. She was as beautiful as ever. Her short, stylish hair was a striking white now, but her blue eyes were as sharp as they always were. She wore the diamond stud earrings he'd given her for Christmas and some kind of loungy outfit of soft black pants and a pale gray top that was loose enough to hide what he knew was a body she kept in excellent shape. But the look in her pretty eyes was as frustrating as the rest of his day had been.

"How can I let it go?" He walked over, dropped onto the couch beside her and fixed his gaze on hers. "That boy was supposed to take over Barrett Toys. He was my future and, now, he's turned his back on everything to get kids hooked on technology."

She laughed, reached over to the closest table for her glass of red wine and took a sip. "You sound like a man on a horse-drawn cart complaining that his son wants one of those newfangled cars."

"Not the same thing at all," he muttered, looking into his scotch glass as if searching for answers.

"Exactly the same." She straightened one leg and used her foot to nudge his thigh. "When you took over from your father, don't you remember how he lamented the end of the company because you wanted to make too many changes?"

He dropped one hand to her foot and lazily stroked it. That was different. His father had been stuck in the mud. No vision. No ability to *listen.* "Yes, but I didn't leave the company, did I?"

"And Luke won't either."

He snapped her a hard look. "He already has."

Loretta waved that away. "He'll be back."

"You sound damn sure of yourself."

"Not of me," she said. "I'm sure of Luke. Yes, he's off on his own right now, but that's not saying he'll stay there."

"If you'd heard him yesterday, you'd believe it."

"He needs to prove himself. Just as much as you needed the same thing about fifty years ago." She sighed a little. "He's as stubborn as you are. That's why the two of you butt heads so often."

"Thanks very much."

She ignored that and wiggled her foot. "Foot rub, please."

He snorted, but obliged.

Loretta sighed her pleasure, but then kept talking. "Like I said, Luke's proving something to you, I think. And until you can accept his ideas and trust him to do the right thing, neither of you is going to be happy. Meanwhile, until Luke comes back, you have Cole to help you out at the company."

"Cole." Shaking his head, Jamison said, "He just doesn't have the head for the company like Luke does. Today, Cole left early again. Took a lunch and then just went home rather than back to work. Said he had some to-do with Susan and Oliver." He paused before demanding, "What kind of activity does a two-year-old have that a father can't miss?"

She gave him a push with her foot. "That two-year-old is our great-grandson."

"And I love him, but Cole's not just that boy's father, he's a vice president of the company…"

"Spending time with his son is a good thing, Jamie."

"I know that, and it's not about that, really. In a family business, you should be able to take off time when you need to, to be with your kids. That's not what really bothers me." Shaking his head again, he muttered, "He doesn't give a flying damn about the business. Meetings at work, he's not paying attention. He's…indifferent. At the heart of it, he doesn't understand or care about what happens to the company and makes no effort to, either. He's just—"

"Just what?"

He looked at her and admitted the truth. "He's not *Luke*."

Studying him, she asked, "This isn't just about Cole's lack of vision and effort or even about Luke, is it? I mean, you're angry and hurt, but there's something else, too."

He scowled at her. "It's not easy being married to a mind reader."

"Thankfully, you have years of practice. So, stop stalling and spill it."

He rubbed at the spot between his eyes but didn't bother trying to ignore her. Jamison knew better than to evade anything as far as his wife was concerned. "I'm losing it, Loretta."

"What do you mean?"

He pushed her foot off his lap and stood up, clutching his scotch glass. "I mean, I'm forgetting things. It's been going on for a while, but lately, it seems to be getting worse."

She frowned a bit, but her voice was soft and easy as she asked, "What kind of things?"

One of the reasons he loved her as fiercely today as he had sixty years before was her inherent calm. Nothing shook the woman. Even when they'd lost both of their sons and daughters-in-law in one blindingly horrific plane crash, she'd been rocked only for a while. Because she had taken her pain and turned it into love she lavished on their grandsons, Cole and Luke.

Jamison was very glad of her stoicism today because by God, he needed it.

"Today, I couldn't find the statistics I had Donna print out for me on the new toy line. I put them on my desk and then a half hour later, they weren't there." Shaking his head, he muttered, "I must have moved them, but damned if I can remember doing it."

"Maybe Donna moved them."

"She said no."

"Well then, you were busy. Distracted."

"Maybe." Distraction only worked as an excuse for so long, though. And he'd been losing track of little things for weeks now. When would that change to the *big* things? Would he forget who he was? Forget Loretta? He ran one hand across the back of his neck and tried to still his racing thoughts. If there was one thing that terrified Jamison, it was the threat of losing *himself.* Of his mind slowly disappearing.

At eighty, he'd prided himself on staying in shape, but there was nothing he could do about his memory. His ideas. His thoughts. If he lost all of that...

"You're worrying for nothing," Loretta said.

"It's not just the statistic reports," he countered. "Yesterday, after Cole and Susan went home, I couldn't find my damn car keys."

"That's not a new phenomenon," Loretta said wryly. "On our first date, you couldn't find them either, remember? You had to walk me home?"

He remembered and his smile proved it. "That was different. I did that on purpose to get more time with you."

"Jamison Barrett!" She slapped his arm. "I got in trouble for that because I was home so late."

"It was worth it," he said with a wink.

Her mouth worked as if she was biting back words trying to slip out. Finally, though, she admitted, "Yes, it was worth it. And, Jamie, you're worried now for nothing. You don't have Alzheimer's. You've just got too much on your mind."

"It's been happening for weeks, Loretta." He scowled at the admission. He hadn't wanted to worry her. Hadn't wanted to acknowledge that there might actually be something to worry about.

"You should have told me."

"I didn't want to talk about it. Now..."

"If you're that worried, go see Dr. Tucker."

His scowl deepened. "That's just admitting that I'm worried."

"You're driving yourself crazy over *nothing*, Jamie. I would have noticed if there was something wrong with you."

A splash of color from the stained-glass window fell on her, shading her hair and her features with pale, rosy light. He looked into her eyes and chose to believe her—because he needed to.

"You're probably right."

She laughed shortly, reaching up to cup his cheek. "After nearly sixty years together, you should know that I'm *always* right."

"True." He smiled. "What was I thinking?"

She moved into him, wrapped her arms around his waist and laid her head on his chest.

He tucked her in close with one arm across her shoulders and took the comfort she offered. And he thanked whatever lucky stars had given him this woman to go through life with. He'd needed this time with Loretta. This calm, soothing time when he could center himself again.

Which was why he didn't mention hiring the woman Donna had told him about.

Fiona stepped out of the shower the next morning and asked herself what the heck she was doing. She and Luke had spent the evening together, and then made plans to tour the city today.

"Shouldn't be doing this," she muttered. "Not supposed to be getting involved in a case. But how can

I not? I have to talk to him, right?" And she really liked him, too. Which made all of this even harder.

"But at the same time, I have to get him to see his grandfather's side of things. Get him to talk to me about this, so I can present arguments he might listen to. Make him want to go back to the business, and I can't do that if I avoid him, right?"

Fiona turned the hot water off and took a second to just rest her forehead against the tiled wall. She'd flown all the way to San Francisco to meet him. To convince him... She couldn't exactly do that if she didn't spend time with him.

She flushed, just thinking about what had happened yesterday at their first meeting. She'd never been so blatantly sexual in her life. And wasn't sure how it had happened, beyond the instant attraction she'd felt for him.

"This has the chance of becoming a real mess," she muttered as she reached for a thick white towel and wrapped it around her still-dripping body. She used another one for her hair, then swiped the steamy fog off the mirror. That didn't help, though. Now she had to meet her own gaze and read the trouble in her own eyes.

Her big plan had been to meet him here, at the conference, where he was away from home. Talk to him, get to know him. Not sexually, just...friendly. Then when they got back home, maybe become his friend and ease him into seeing that his grandfather and the family company needed him.

"But I shot that plan down myself." Frowning at her reflection, she said, "This is really not good."

He was her job, damn it. She was supposed to be resolving his life, not throwing her own into turmoil. This was her job, and she was going to be professional. She had no business at all fantasizing about the most gorgeous man she'd ever seen. God, it was just embarrassing what had happened earlier. She never should have fallen into his lap.

When her cell phone rang, she thought of it as a break from her crazy-making thoughts. Then she saw the call screen and sighed. No avoiding this, either.

"Mr. Barrett," she said, forcing a smile into her voice. "I didn't expect to hear from you so soon."

Actually, she'd been hoping she wouldn't. But in her short acquaintance with Luke's grandfather, she'd already learned the older man wasn't exactly patient. Still, she didn't have anything to report. Didn't have any news to give him. And she couldn't exactly share with the man that his grandson had set her body on fire.

"Ms. Jordan—is it all right if I call you Fiona?"

"Of course." She straightened the tower of a towel on her head, then with one hand, wiped the steam off the mirror again.

"Did you meet with Luke?"

"I did," she said, though she wouldn't be telling him how that first meeting had gone. She could just imagine. God, that would be mortifying. Yeah. That would be good.

Keep your mind off Luke. At least while you're talking to his grandfather.

"I'm meeting him in an hour. We're going to spend the day together." And she hoped to be able to get him talking about his grandfather again. Get this job back on track. Jamison Barrett had hired her to bring his grandson back into the family business, and she was going to do it. She'd never failed on a contract before, and she wouldn't this time, either.

Fiona's business, ICanFixIt, had been born out of her innate ability to solve problems. Not math, of course. Math was terrifying to her. But if someone lost a diamond ring, or a puppy, she could find it. If you needed tickets to a sold-out concert, Fiona could get them. Find long-lost relatives, she was your girl. Basically, Fiona could fix your problem, no matter what it was.

So, she wouldn't spoil her success record by failing this time.

"He's ignoring the conference in favor of you?" Jamison chuckled. "I'm impressed. Nothing my boy likes better than the technology business and being around others just like him. You must be a miracle worker after all."

"I wouldn't say that," she said, and frowned at her reflection.

"Well, from what my secretary, Donna, tells me, you accomplish the impossible all the time."

She winced. Yes. She had worked for Donna's sister Linda. Fiona had found the daughter Linda had given up for adoption thirty years ago, and she'd helped the two women reunite. Which was how Jamison had found out about Fiona in the first place.

At the time, she'd had no idea that finding a long-lost daughter would be considered easy compared to what she was supposed to do now. From what she'd seen of Luke yesterday, not only was he gorgeous, ridiculously sexy and funny on top of it…he was also stubborn and determined to make his own company take off. She was on his side in that because she knew just how much her business meant to her.

But Jamison was her client, so her loyalties had to be to him.

"Mr. Barrett, I don't want you to get your hopes up too high," she warned quietly. Yes, she'd never failed before, but what was it her foster mom had always told her? *There's always a first time.* "I'm going to do my best, but your grandson seems very stubborn."

"He is," Jamison grumbled. "Got that from his grandmother."

Fiona almost laughed aloud at that. It was clear to her that Luke was more like his grandfather than either man would probably admit.

"This is the last night of the conference," he said next. "Luke will be flying home tomorrow, so I'll expect another update from you tomorrow night or the following morning at the latest."

"Of course," she said, and silently hoped that she would have some good news to give him. But from what she'd seen of Luke Barrett so far, Fiona had the feeling he wasn't the kind of man to make hasty decisions. He'd left the family business because he was convinced that it was the right move for him.

How was she supposed to change his mind over the course of a single weekend? Answer? She couldn't. It was going to take more than this weekend, which meant that she'd be seeing lots more of Luke Barrett.

She looked into the mirror and saw eager anticipation in her own eyes. Oh, not good.

"Fine, then. I look forward to hearing from you. Get it done." Jamison hung up a moment later, and Fiona set her phone down.

Staring at the woman in the mirror, she said, "This is just another job, Fiona."

When her own reflection rolled her eyes at that, Fiona knew she was in deep doo-doo. "No getting involved. No letting your hormones drive the car here. Get Luke talking about his family. Make him realize what he's walking away from. And when it's over...*you* walk away. Because if Luke discovers you were hired to meet him, convince him, he'll never speak to you again anyway."

So, it would be better for her if she simply didn't get attached in the first place...

By that evening, Luke felt like he was standing at the edge of a very high cliff. His body had been tight and hard since the moment Fiona had dropped into his lap the day before. Ditching the conference and spending time with her instead hadn't helped the situation any.

They'd played tourist all day, taking a cab down Lombard Street, checking out Golden Gate Park and stopping for a drink at a tiny pub at Fisherman's Wharf. Hell, if anyone had told him a week ago that he'd be playing tourist, he'd have laughed in their face.

But Fiona had wanted to see the park and the wharf, so he'd gone along. She'd checked out the sights and he'd watched *her*. The night before, his sleep had been haunted by images of her and now he had even more memories to draw on. Fiona, standing at the rail on the wharf as a sea wind tossed her hair and lifted that short black skirt. Her grin as their driver took them down the most notoriously twisted street in the world.

Not to mention the way her tongue had caressed the ice cream cone he'd bought her at the park.

He briefly closed his eyes and muffled a groan at *that* thought.

To distract himself while he sat in the bar and waited for Fiona to arrive for their dinner date, he opened his phone and checked his email. There were twenty new messages to go through and as he did, Luke shut out the rest of the room as if he were alone on an island.

The truth was, if he hadn't met Fiona, he'd have been bored out of his mind.

This conference had nothing new to offer him. Luke had already chosen his path, knew his own plans and had no interest in making changes to what was, in effect, a newborn company. He'd only come to San Francisco because he'd felt that he should make an appearance, talk to a couple of old friends. Then he'd met Fiona. She'd shaken him and he had no problem admitting that—at least to himself. She was smart and funny and confident and all three of those things, combined with that body and those eyes, had his mind wandering even while dealing with email.

"Not good." Luke shook his head to clear it. He had enough going on in his life right now and definitely didn't need the distraction of a woman—even one as intriguing as Fiona. Hell, he thought, maybe especially not one as intriguing as Fiona.

He had to focus on his company. No time in his life at the moment for a woman like her.

Blowing out a breath, he read the message from his assistant, Jack.

We've hit a snag in early production, boss. Peterson says they're backlogged and won't get to do the run of our new tablets in time for a Christmas release.

"Well, damn it." Frustration roared through him. Yes, to anyone else, talking about Christmas releases in February sounded ridiculous. But these things were always planned out months, if not years, in advance. Usually for just this reason. Something always went wrong.

This wasn't the first time Luke had had to deal with wrenches thrown into the works. At Barrett Toys and Tech, they'd often had to pull off last-minute miracles. Yes, his cousin Cole had supposedly been in charge of taking care of their production partners, but more often than not, that job had fallen to Luke. He'd handle it this time, too. Quickly, he fired off an email to Jack.

Tell Peterson we have a contract, and I expect him to honor it. Tell him I said to find a way. If he gives you any crap, I'll take care of it myself on Monday.

That would probably be enough to keep the man on track. If it wasn't, Luke would find someone else to do the job and word would spread that Peterson's Manufacturing couldn't be trusted to honor its schedules.

Focused now on his business, he answered a few more emails from marketing, engineering and design, then skipped the one from his grandfather. He knew damn well that Jamison would be telling him again that he should come back to the family business.

A quick ping of regret echoed inside him, but he ignored it. He loved that old man, but damned if he'd go back where his opinions weren't trusted. His new business wasn't just a company but a matter of pride. Luke wasn't going to walk away from it.

"Excuse me?"

A woman's voice from right beside him. One of the waitresses had already tried to freshen his drink twice before. He waved one hand at the table. "I don't need a refill, thanks."

"Good to know," the woman said, then added, "So do I have to fall into your lap again to get your attention?"

He went still before turning his head to look up at Fiona. If he'd thought she was stunning earlier in that short, flirty skirt, it was nothing to what he was thinking now.

She wore a dark red, off-the-shoulder dress that defined every curve in her body like a lover's hands. The dress was nipped in tightly at her narrow waist and the short, tight skirt stopped midway on her thighs. The black heels completed her outfit and made her legs look amazing. Instantly, he had a mental image of those legs locked around his hips while she pulled him deeper inside her heat.

And…just like that, he was too hard to stand.

Her hair was pulled back into a low ponytail that hung between her shoulders and her coffee-colored eyes sparkled as if she knew exactly what effect she was having on him.

"Have you seen enough?" she asked, "or would you like me to do a slow turn?"

If he saw her butt in that dress, it would finish him off. "Not necessary. Have a seat."

"Oh." She glanced toward the dining room. "I thought we were going to dinner. I am sort of hungry."

"Right. Carnivore. I remember." He nodded and as she sat down, he signaled for the waitress. "But that's going to have to wait until I can walk again."

Her mouth curved and he wanted nothing more than to taste it. "Again?" She smiled. "You're really good for my self-esteem."

"Yeah. Happy to help…" When the waitress arrived, Fiona looked up at her.

"Vodka martini, please. Dirty."

When they were alone again, Luke finished off the email he'd been composing. Anything to get his mind off what his mind wanted to stay on.

"Are we having a phone date?" Fiona asked, and her voice was so soft and sultry, he had to look up and meet her eyes.

"Should I get mine out of my purse?" She reached for the small black clutch she'd set on the table a moment ago.

"What? No. Just a little business I have to take care of."

"Uh-huh."

The waitress returned, set a chilled cocktail glass in front of Fiona and left again. Taking the stirrer from the glass, Fiona ate one of the three olives, then took a sip. "So business, anytime, anywhere?"

He tore his gaze from the email and glanced at her again, just in time to watch her put the second olive in her mouth and slide the stirrer between her lips.

Luke took a deep breath. "It's important."

"Oh, I'm sure." She sat back in the black leather

chair and sipped at her drink. "Do you always do business after business hours?"

A little irritated with himself at how easily Fiona affected him, Luke concentrated on composing the email. "When I have to."

"You were working yesterday afternoon when we met, too."

"Things have to get done, whether I'm at the company or away."

"But today, you almost never checked your phone."

"Making up for it now," he said. It had been years since he'd gone most of the day without checking emails. But he hadn't been able to take his eyes off of her. It wasn't just a sexual pull he felt for her. He actually enjoyed listening to her, talking to her. It had been a long time since a woman had captivated him like this.

And right now, for Luke, that was off-limits. Fiona wasn't the kind of woman you walked away from easily. So, it was better to not get involved at all, right?

"So, you're never really off duty?"

"Not usually." He hit Send, and a response to his earlier message to Jack arrived. Dutifully, he clicked on it and smiled in satisfaction.

"What's the point in having your own business if you never have any time off?"

He lifted his gaze to hers and reached for his

drink. "Clearly, you don't know how much is involved in running your own business."

"Not true. I just don't let my business interfere with my *life*."

He snorted. "This business *is* my life."

"Well, that's just sad," Fiona mused.

Luke stared at her. "Sad? I'm building a company from the ground up. That's not sad. It's exciting. Challenging."

"And sucking up everything around it like a black hole?"

He laughed shortly, looked back at the email he was writing to Jack. He finished it off, hit Send and then set his phone on the table beside him.

"Amazing," he said. "For a second there, you almost sounded like my grandfather."

Her eyebrows arched. "What every woman longs to hear."

"Not what I meant." Luke shook his head. "It's just that he's suddenly anti-technology."

"Oh, then I'm not like him at all," Fiona said, sipping at her drink again. "I like technology. I love email and texting with my mom who makes hilarious typos, and I'm very fond of my washing machine, car and television."

Nodding, he smiled. "Glad to hear it. That's what people don't get—including my grandfather. Tech isn't just computers or robots or drones. More than a hundred years ago, tech was the first airplane. It's about the future. Seeing it. Grabbing it."

"What about the present?"

"What?"

"The present," she repeated, giving him a knowing smile. "As in dinner? Can you walk yet?"

"As long as you don't sit on my lap again, I think we're good." He stood up, then walked around the table to pull her chair out.

She slowly rose, took a deep breath that lifted the tops of her breasts to dangerous levels and said, "I'll try to restrain myself."

And it wasn't going to be easy. She didn't have to actually touch him, Luke realized. Just looking at her was enough to feed a fire that threatened to burn him to ash.

Luke steered Fiona toward the hostess, then followed behind as the woman guided them to a table by a wide window. His gaze dropped to Fiona's butt and the way it swayed with her every step. He wanted his hands on her. Soon.

Four

"We've spent the day together and I still don't know why *you're* in San Francisco," Luke said.

True. She'd managed for most of the day to steer the conversation around to him. To keep him talking about his own company and, every once in a while, to bring up the grandfather who was so desperate to get Luke back into the fold.

Because she couldn't tell him what he wanted to know. Couldn't reveal that she had been hired to meet him and ease him back into his family. So, she was left with half-truths and outright lies. Fiona wasn't comfortable with them, but sometimes, there was just no other way.

"I'm actually here on business," she said.

His mesmerizing eyes locked on her, and she just managed not to shiver.

"Who do you work for?"

"Oh, I've got my own business." Fiona reached for her purse. She dug inside for the brightly flowered, metallic card holder that had been a gift from her best friend, Laura. Opening it up, she pulled out a card and handed it to him.

He looked at it and a quizzical expression crossed his face. She couldn't blame him. Most people had that initial reaction.

"ICanFixIt?" He lifted his gaze to hers, and Fiona gave another little jolt. His eyes had a sort of power over her she hadn't really expected—or found a way to combat, yet.

"Fix what?"

She shrugged. "Anything, really. If you need it fixed, I can do it."

He tucked her card into his inner jacket pocket in a move that felt oddly intimate. "That's fairly vague."

"What's vague? Actually, it's a perfect description of what I do."

"Explain."

Well, it wasn't the first time she'd had to give an explanation of what she did. Her business card really said it all.

"If someone's lost something or if they have something they need and can't get, then they call me, and I fix it."

"Easy as that."

It wasn't a question, but at the same time, it was. "I didn't say it was easy." Fiona smiled at him because, honestly, he looked so dubious it was going to be fun to prove him wrong. Plus, she still had flames licking at her insides when she looked into his eyes. There was definitely something happening between them that she hadn't counted on. That she hadn't expected at all. Was it going to complicate the situation? Absolutely. Oh sure, he was paying attention to her and that would help with her goal of convincing him to go back to his family business. But she wasn't a one-night kind of woman and, once he found out she'd set him up from their first meeting, that's all she would be relegated to. Was that going to change how she was feeling? Nope.

"Tell me something you've 'fixed' lately."

"Okay." She did a quick flip through her mental file folders and came up with a quick example.

"About two weeks ago, a woman called me for help finding her son's letterman jacket."

He laughed.

Fiona scowled at him. She wasn't really surprised at his reaction, but she was a little disappointed. Just because it seemed silly to Luke didn't mean that it wasn't important to the kid who'd lost his jacket.

"It seems like a small thing to you, but that boy worked really hard to earn his varsity letter. And his mom paid a lot of money for that jacket. Money she couldn't spare."

"But she could afford to hire you?"

Fiona grinned. "She made her son pay my fee out of his savings."

"Okay." He nodded. "Good for her. So how did you solve the problem?"

Pleased, Fiona continued. "I backtracked. Found out where he'd been, who he'd been with, if he'd stopped anywhere along his route."

He frowned again. "Sounds like a lot of work."

She shrugged that off. "You work hard, don't you?"

"Of course."

"So do I. Anyway," she said, "I went everywhere that Ryder went over a long weekend, because he couldn't remember where he was the last time he'd seen the jacket."

"Of course he couldn't."

She ignored that. "Really, it's amazing how many places a teenager can go in one weekend." Smiling now, she said, "I went to a hamburger stand in Bolsa Chica, a surf shop in Huntington Beach, a movie theater in Newport and a shake shack in Laguna. He was also applying for some jobs, so that took me back to Long Beach and then Palos Verdes, and I really hate driving over the Vincent Thomas Bridge."

He laughed again. "Why?"

"It's *huge*," she said. "Really long and really high, and I drive a Volkswagen Bug so when a truck gets close, I just picture myself sailing over the edge."

"You won't go over the edge. The railings are too high."

"Okay, then, being crushed."

"Reasonable," he admitted.

"Thank you." How very *kind* of him to admit she had a right to be nervous. A little irritated in spite of her attraction to him, she went on. "So, I talked to dozens of people, went through a lot of lost-and-found boxes, and finally found the jacket."

"I admit it. I'm intrigued. Where'd you find it?"

"At a girl's house." Grinning, Fiona picked up the martini she'd carried with her to the dining room and took a sip. "She'd seen the boy at a coffee shop in Long Beach where he was applying for a job. She goes to school with him, has a huge crush on him, and when he forgot the jacket after his interview, she picked it up."

"She just took it?" His expression said he was appalled.

"Well, she said she had completely planned to give it back to him at school, but instead, she held on to it. I do think she was going to give it back eventually, she just liked having it."

"So she stole it."

Fiona held up one finger for correction. "She rescued it."

"And held it hostage."

Laughing, Fiona shook her head. "There was no ransom, and I really think you're missing the point of this."

"Fine. Clue me in."

"The point is, I found the jacket. I returned it to the boy and his very grateful mother."

"And did you tell him about the girl who had it?"

Fiona winced. "Since she pleaded with me not to, no. I didn't. She was embarrassed."

"She was a thief."

Fiona tipped her head to one side and studied him. This was a side of him she hadn't seen before. Until now, he'd been charming, funny and just sexy as hell. His response now, though, painted a hard, unforgiving picture that was a little startling. "That's cold."

"Just a fact." He shrugged. "She took it and didn't return it."

"She was going to." Fiona was sure of it. Heck, she remembered being in high school and completely infatuated with the star of the baseball team. Who had, naturally, not been aware of her existence. She had understood what the girl was thinking, and Fiona had believed her when she'd sworn that she was going to give the jacket back. "So to you, facts are all that matter? No straying from the straight and narrow?"

"Is that so unusual? You're okay with people stealing things?"

"Of course not, but I'm willing to admit that people do things they regret—"

"Everyone does." His features darkened for a moment before he said, "Doesn't mean you don't have to accept the consequences."

"I'm all about responsibility, but a little understanding wouldn't hurt, either."

"Right and wrong. Period." He sipped at his

drink and looked completely at ease with that pronouncement.

Well, that didn't bode well for her, Fiona thought. She'd started this—whatever it was between them— with a lie. She doubted he'd understand that.

"So, no shades of gray in your world?"

He shook his head. "Not really."

"Must be difficult being perfect in an imperfect world."

His lips curved briefly. "I didn't say I was perfect. When I'm wrong, I own it."

Her guess was, he didn't consider himself wrong very often. "And do you confess it?"

He didn't say anything, and Fiona could guess what that meant. No, he didn't. She imagined that apologies didn't come easy to a man so sure he was right all the time. So she used that moment to drive home her point. "Then why should this girl confess? Or have what she did pointed out? Who would gain? I returned the jacket. The boy was happy. His mom was happy. And the girl doesn't have to be worried about being teased or bullied at school over it."

"And did she learn anything?"

"I think so." In fact, she was sure of it. Fiona remembered the horrified expression on the girl's face when she'd been tracked down.

"And that's your business?" he asked. "Tracking down jackets stolen by starry-eyed schoolgirls?"

"It's an example." This wasn't the first time someone had been dismissive of her business. But she bristled a little at his tone anyway. Feeling a little defensive now, she said, "I've helped people research their thesis, found a lost engagement ring, arranged for a band for a wedding and just a couple of months ago, I reunited a woman with the daughter she gave up for adoption thirty years ago."

And that case was the main reason she was here today. Of course, she couldn't tell Luke that. He might put things together if he found out that Fiona had done work for the sister of his grandfather's secretary.

His eyebrows arched. "That's impressive."

"Thank you. I know to some, my business might sound silly or not worth doing, even." Lifting her martini for another sip, she let the icy liquid cool the bubbles of insult in the pit of her stomach. It was ridiculous to take offense at Luke's remarks or outlook. It didn't matter what he thought of her business, did it? She'd faced the same thing from a lot of people over the years. It hadn't changed anything for Fiona.

She had a skill that she'd used in high school to make friends and, once grown, she'd honed her talents into a business that served a real purpose, and Fiona was proud of what she'd built. As proud, she was willing to bet, as Luke was of his tech business.

"But when it's your engagement ring that's missing, it's a big deal. Or when you manage to surprise your grandmother with tickets to a play she's been wanting to see." Fiona smiled at that memory. "It's not just the big things that are important, right? Sometimes, the small things in life mean the most."

"How did you get started in this 'business'?"

"You don't have to say it like that," she said. "As if it isn't a real company. I'm not as big as Barrett Toys and Tech, but I support myself and provide a service."

He gave her a slow nod. "Understood. So, how did you get started?"

"Kind of a long story…"

"I'll take my chances."

Fiona shrugged. "Okay, then. I grew up in a series of different foster homes." Before he could offer sympathy that she didn't want or need, she rushed on. "So that meant going to strange schools and always being the new girl."

"Rough."

"Especially for a teenager," she agreed, happy he hadn't gotten the pity gleam in his eyes that too many people did when learning about her background. It hadn't been easy, sure. But she'd survived. "So to make friends, I started offering help to people. Dog walking. Babysitting. Finding a pair of lost glasses. Tutoring football players. If it needed doing, I could do it."

He didn't say anything, just kept his gaze on her. She shifted a little uncomfortably under his steady stare but continued. "I went to community college, took business courses and turned my skill into a way to make my living."

"You still dog walking?"

"If someone needs it, sure. I also arrange for DJs for weddings, bounce houses for kids' parties, tours of movie studios…"

"And how do you pull that off?" He was curious, she could see it in his eyes, and she smiled.

"I've got a lot of friends with interesting jobs and we help each other out." She paused, then said, "I know that most of what I do doesn't sound important to you—or anyone else. But it's important to the people who hire me, and isn't that the point?"

He thought about that for a long moment, his gaze locked with hers. "Yes," he finally said. "You're right. It is."

His phone vibrated on the table and sounded like a rattlesnake in the brush. Fiona jumped, then frowned a bit when Luke reached for it. He glanced at the screen.

"This is business, just excuse me for a minute."

Times had changed, she reminded herself. Now no one thought twice about taking phone calls during dinner, or at a play or in the movies. And watching Luke, she could see his grandfather's point. Sure, technology was a great thing to have. It kept people connected—but it also had the ability to isolate them. If someone was more interested in a phone conversation than talking to the person he was with, why be with another person at all?

In spite of her annoyance, Luke's deep, rumbling voice sent shivers along her spine. His expressions shifted according to whatever the caller had to say. She could barely hear him, so she had no idea what the conversation was about. All she knew was that she was sitting opposite a gorgeous man who was more interested in his phone than in her. In the long run, that was probably best, she told herself. After all, she wasn't trying to make a romantic connection. She looked around the elegant dining room and saw that most of the people were staring at their phones.

It was a plague, she thought suddenly. And she was sympathetic to his grandfather's efforts to fight it... Strange that she'd never really paid all that much attention to people's dependency on technology until accepting this job from Jamison Barrett. She'd never paid much attention to people's love of technology simply because she was usually too busy. The evidence had been all around her all the time. Heck, she'd no doubt been guilty of it herself. Until today. As she sat there, waiting for Luke to hang up and look at her again, Fiona realized that she really liked him. Which had not been in the plan at all.

When Luke hung up, she said, "I propose a phone ban."

"Excuse me?"

"No more phones tonight. You took two calls earlier and now this one." Shrugging, she said, "I suggest we both put our phones on the table and the first one to reach for it loses."

"Loses what?"

"The agreement."

His eyes sparked and she saw a definite gleam there that kindled the fires inside her to burn hotter and higher. Apparently, Luke Barrett thrived on competition.

"And what does the winner get?"

"Hmm. Good question. The pride of knowing they won?"

"Not much of an inducement to get me to ignore business calls," he said.

What would be enough? she wondered. She couldn't offer a cash prize because he was a billionaire; he wouldn't need her twenty bucks. Then an idea occurred to her that stirred up the flames inside to make them bright enough to read by.

"Okay," she countered as a dangerous thought occurred to her. "A kiss."

Well, she had his attention anyway. Kissing Luke Barrett was more tempting than she wanted to admit even to herself. And maybe that's why she'd suggested the prize. After all, she knew very well, that whatever was between she and Luke now, it wasn't going to go anywhere, so why not a kiss?

"One kiss?" He lifted an eyebrow, and she wondered how he did that. "One kiss isn't much of a prize."

"It is if you know what you're doing," she said.

His eyes darkened until they were the color of a stormy sea. "A challenge. I like it."

"So you agree? No phone. Winner gets a kiss."

"Then the loser gets one, too."

"True, but—"

"But," he said, "the winner chooses where, when, for how long and how deep."

Just hearing him say those words set up a low, throbbing ache and made her heart quicken into a beat that was wild and fierce.

And that was just *talking* about a kiss. Maybe this wasn't a very good idea.

"Deal?" He set his phone on the tabletop.

Fiona had one last chance to back out, but somehow, she just couldn't. Instead, she laid her phone beside his and the challenge began.

Dinner was good, but Luke hardly tasted it. All he could think of was the kiss that was coming his way. He'd wanted to taste her since the moment they'd met, and now it was so close, his mind was completely fixated.

His phone buzzed again. Third time in the last half hour, and he didn't even look at it. Instead, he met her gaze and saw the smile in those brown depths. She fully expected him to cave. To take the call, because she'd been seeing him do just that too many times. But Fiona Jordan had no idea just how determined he could be when he was focused on a goal.

And tonight, *she* was the goal. A temporary distraction? When he was back home, he could focus on his company. Here...

"I'm sorry to interrupt..."

Luke turned to look at a tall blonde woman in a slinky black dress standing beside a little boy clutching a stuffed green alligator to his chest.

After a brief glance at Luke, the woman looked at Fiona and smiled. "I'm really sorry, we'll only be a minute."

"It's no problem, Shelley," Fiona said, then looked down at the little boy. "Hi, Jake."

"Tank oo." He gave her a shy smile, snuggling up to his mom's leg as he rubbed his alligator across his cheek. "You find Dragon."

"Well, you're very welcome," Fiona told him with a grin. "He looks so happy now to be back with you."

Jake gave her a wide, two-year-old's smile and hugged the threadbare stuffed animal a little harder. "Me, too."

"I'm glad."

"He wanted to say thank you himself," Jake's mother said, "so when we saw you in the dining room, we had to come over."

"It's not a problem. I was happy to help."

"You have no idea how much you helped." Shelley smoothed one hand over her son's tousled blond hair. "He was heartbroken because Dragon was lost. He couldn't even sleep last night."

"Tank oo," the boy said again, then turned and scampered back to the table where his father sat, holding a baby girl with a bright pink ribbon in her hair.

"Seriously, thank you." Shelley shook Fiona's hand and left.

"Another satisfied client?"

Fiona smiled. "Jake lost Dragon yesterday somewhere in the hotel and, today, I saw his mom searching for it. But she was holding her baby and Jake was crying in his father's arms, so I volunteered to find it."

He frowned as he glanced at the happy little boy

again. "We were together all day. When did you do this?"

She waved one hand. "When I went upstairs to change for dinner, I met up with them in the elevator."

Luke thought back. "You were only gone forty-five minutes. You found it that quickly?"

"This one was easy," she said. "They'd been at the pool most of the day, so I checked and found out the towels had been taken to the hotel laundry right after the family left the pool. Turns out, Dragon got lost in a bunch of towels. So, I went down there, and they let me look through the gigantic tubs of damp towels from the pool area that hadn't been washed yet and I found him." She shrugged. "No big deal."

Luke looked back to where the little boy was sitting, holding tightly to his alligator, and then turned his gaze back to Fiona. "To Jake it was."

She beamed at him. "You get it."

"Yeah," he said, now more determined than ever to win their bet because there was nothing he wanted more than to kiss her senseless. To lose himself in her. "I think I do."

Her phone rang, a medieval-sounding tune, and still smiling, she automatically reached for it.

"You lose," Luke said.

She stopped, hand poised above her phone. The music finally ended as the call went to voice mail, but it was too late, and they both knew it. "Not fair. I was distracted."

Luke smiled, looked her dead in the eye and whispered, "Not nearly as much as you're going to be."

The promise of a kiss hung over the rest of their dinner date, and by the time they were finished and the bill was paid, Luke was strung tighter than a harp string. He'd never looked forward so much to a damn kiss. Hell, he'd been torturing himself since the moment she'd dropped into his lap. Knowing that he was finally going to get a taste of her was pushing him closer and closer to the edge.

"You know, we should probably talk about this..."

He had one hand at the small of her back, and he could have sworn he felt heat pouring from her body into his. "You're not trying to back out, are you? This was your idea."

They walked out onto the wide flagstone patio and walkway that wended its way through a gigantic garden before winding around the hotel itself.

"Yes, but—"

"But you thought you'd win," he finished for her and saw her mouth work as if she were biting back what she wanted to say. "Admit it. You thought I'd cave and grab for my phone."

"Well, of course I did," she said, tossing a quick look up at him. "Who knew you could be so..."

"Determined? Strong? Single-minded?"

"All of the above."

He grinned and kept her walking until they were in the deserted garden. The wind was whipping in off the ocean, and February in San Francisco could be downright cold. It seemed no one else was willing to brave the chill and that suited Luke just fine.

"It was a silly bet," she said.

"And yet we made it."

She stopped, looked up at him and narrowed her eyes. "You're enjoying this, aren't you?"

"So much," he admitted. He smiled at her, but that smile slowly dissolved as he *really* looked at her. That long dark hair was lifting in the wind and her brown eyes looked almost black in the moonlight.

If Luke had been looking for a romantic setting, he couldn't have picked a better spot. Trees swaying, flowers scenting the air, and the moon, shining out of a cloud swept sky, painting shadows on the grass. There were a few old-fashioned lamps made to look like gaslights sprinkled throughout the garden, adding splashes of gold in the darkness.

But it wasn't romance he was after, he reminded himself. He wasn't looking for a relationship, just to quench the fires inside. Lust was driving him. Pure need and a desire so all-consuming, he'd never known anything like it before.

"Are you trying to back out of our deal?" he asked quietly, keeping his gaze locked on hers so he could see if there was the slightest hesitation there.

"That would be awkward, since it was my idea in the first place."

"Not an answer," he said, his voice deepening with the need clawing at his throat. Still watching her eyes, he saw desire, irritation at herself for losing this little bet, but he didn't see "no." *Thank God.*

"No, I'm not trying to back out," she said, and took a deep breath as if steeling herself for a challenge. "You won, so it's your call. Just as we agreed."

He reached for her and slid his hands up and down her arms until she shivered under his touch. Her tongue swept out to lick her bottom lip, and everything in Luke fisted tight.

"I suppose if I were a gentleman, I'd let you squirm out of this…"

"But you're not a gentleman, are you?" she asked, tossing her wind-blown hair back from her face.

"Nope," he whispered, bending his head to hers.

"I'm glad," she murmured just before his mouth took hers.

The moment their mouths met, Luke knew he'd never be satisfied with a single kiss. The taste of her swamped him, filling every cell, flavoring his breath, fogging his mind.

She swayed into him and his arms came around her, one hand sweeping up her back to cradle her head in his palm. His fingers threaded through her hair, he held her still so he could drown in the sensation of having her with him at last.

It had been the longest day or two in his life. Being constantly tortured at her presence and not touching her had driven him crazy. And now he was determined to make the most of the kiss she'd lost to him.

Their tongues tangled together, and he swallowed

her sigh. He devoured her, feeding the need within and spiking it to heights he hadn't known existed. She was more than he'd expected. More than he'd thought possible. And a part of him realized that made her dangerous to a man who wasn't interested in anything that lasted longer than a couple of weeks.

Who would have guessed she would be so addictive? The taste of her. The feel of her body, pliant and giving, pinned to his. The slide of her hair against his hand and the sound of her sighs. Everything about her demanded that he take his time. Everything he was told him to stop now while he still could.

Regretfully, Luke drew his head back and stared down at her. Her eyes were closed, her mouth still ready for the kiss to continue. Her breath heaved in and out of her lungs, and he saw her pounding pulse in the elegant column of her throat.

He couldn't seem to let her go. Her heat called to him. The need still gripping him erupted into a throbbing ache in his dick. All he could think about was sliding her dress down her shoulders, so he could bare her breasts to him. But damned if he'd act like a horny teenager in a public garden.

Slowly, she opened her eyes and looked up at him. Her tongue crossed her top lip, and she gave him such a sensuous, deliberate look, it was all Luke could do to keep from tasting her again.

"Wow."

He snorted. "Wow?"

Fiona took a deep breath, giving him a glimpse

of her cleavage that only deepened the ache he felt. "Well, yeah. That was a really good kiss."

Luke grinned. No games. No playing or trying to pretend that kiss hadn't shaken both of them. Damned if he didn't like Fiona Jordan almost as much as he wanted her.

"Thanks," he said wryly, lifting one hand to stroke his fingertips along her cheek. "I try."

She patted his chest, then swept both hands through her hair. Taking another deep breath as if to steady herself, she blew it out in a rush. "It's appreciated. Seriously. So. Deal honored?"

Best bet he'd ever made. "Yeah."

"Then what do we do now?"

Images filled his mind, and heat roared through his bloodstream. He shoved them all aside, hoping she was thinking the same things. "Your call."

She looked up at him, smiled and said, "Ice cream."

"What?" That was so far off from where his mind was that he didn't know how to process it for a second or two. She went from a passion-fueled kiss hot enough to consume them both to...*ice cream*?

"I saw a great-looking creamery just a block or so from here."

Luke really didn't know what the hell to make of Fiona. He liked her. He wanted her. He worried about getting too close to her. But following her train of thought wasn't easy.

Still. Maybe ice cream would freeze the fires inside. Worth a shot.

Five

A couple of hours later, Fiona heard her best friend answer the phone and blurted out, "Help me."

"Who is this?"

Fiona choked out a laugh. "Laura, not kidding. I think I'm in deep trouble here."

Laura's tone changed instantly from teasing to worried. "What's wrong?"

Sighing a little, Fiona smiled to herself. She knew she could count on Laura Baker. Laura and her husband, Mike, owned the Long Beach duplex where Fiona lived. The Bakers had the three-bedroom unit and Fiona was up front in the one bedroom. From the moment Fiona had moved in a few years ago, the two women had bonded as if they'd known each other their entire lives.

And for Fiona that was a gift like nothing she'd ever known before. Oh, she had a huge circle of "friends" that she'd deliberately made along the way, to somehow fill the emptiness that never having a family of her own had carved into her heart. But finding Laura was like living her whole life alone and suddenly discovering she had a sister.

Like she'd told Luke, she'd grown up in a series of foster homes, bouncing like the proverbial Ping-Pong ball throughout Orange County. Until she was sixteen and was sent to Julie Maxwell. Julie was more than a foster mom. She had become *Mom.* She'd given Fiona the stability and sense of belonging that she'd always dreamed of. And when Fiona aged out of the system, Julie had insisted that she stay on at the house and go to school. Julie was the only real mother Fiona had ever known and she'd always be grateful.

She was just as thankful to have Laura in her life. Laura was short, blonde and, as her husband liked to say, *stacked.* She was also the most sensible human Fiona had ever known and the first one she went to with a problem. And she had a beauty to talk about this time.

"It's Luke Barrett. He's too sexy."

Laura laughed. "Is that even possible? Isn't that like too skinny? Too rich? Who ever heard of too sexy?"

Mike shouted in the background, "Thanks, babe!"

"Wasn't talking to you," Laura called back with a laugh, then asked Fiona, "What's going on?"

Fiona clutched the phone and paced aimlessly. Standing in this beautiful hotel room, all alone, she imagined that she was sitting next to Laura on her big leather sofa and immediately felt better. She stopped at the windows and stared out at San Francisco, draped in lights that made the city look magical at night. "This job. It's not turning out like I thought it would."

"Hold on." Then she called out to her husband. "Mike, bring me a glass of wine, will you?" Back to Fiona, she said, "I'm thinking I'm going to need one. Am I wrong?"

"Tell him to bring the bottle."

"Well, now I'm intrigued. Okay, I've got my wine. Travis is tucked into bed. I'm all yours. Talk."

So she did. While she continued to pace like a tiger in a too-small cage, Fiona told Laura everything that had happened from the moment she'd dropped into Luke's lap. Through it all, Laura only gave a murmured "Oooh" and a few sighs.

Finally, Fiona told her about the kiss that had singed every nerve ending she had and ended up with, "What do I do now?"

"Have sex?" Laura asked.

"Great idea!" Mike shouted, his voice coming clearly through the phone.

Fiona laughed again and felt the tight knot in her chest begin to dissolve. This is what she'd needed.

To talk it all out with Laura. To be back in her "normal" zone. "I can't. It wouldn't be ethical. Would it?"

"Ethics, schmethics," Laura said. "Is he married?"

"No!"

"You're not either. So, what's the problem?"

"Um…" Fiona waved one hand in the air. "How about I'm lying to him? I'm working for his grandfather. This whole trip was paid for by Jamison Barrett just so I could convince Luke to go back to the family business."

"And did you take a celibacy pledge when I wasn't looking?"

"No, but—"

"Are you hoping that he's *the one* and you'll find happily-ever-after with him?"

Okay, she could admit that it wouldn't have taken much to imagine a perfect future with Luke as a gorgeous husband and father to a few beautiful kids. But that wasn't the point. Because the chances of anything like that happening were *way* out there.

"No, of course not, but—"

"Do you want him?"

Easy question to answer, given that her blood was still burning, and she could still taste his mouth on hers. "Oh, yes."

"So stop being so tortured. Go to bed with the man. Enjoy yourself." Laura took a breath, then said, "Let's face it. He's going to be furious when he finds out what's going on anyway. You've already said there's no future with the guy. So why not have the memory of great sex to help you through it?"

"Maybe he won't find out," Fiona argued. And really, if the job went well, he shouldn't. He should just go back to the family business and pick up his life without ever knowing that the woman he spent a long weekend with was the reason why he'd changed his life around.

"He'll find out, sweetie," Laura said. "If you want something to stay secret, that's practically a guarantee that it won't."

"That's helpful." Fiona frowned as she caught her own reflection in the window glass. She hated the idea of Luke thinking she was a liar. That she'd felt nothing for him. Because despite her best efforts to remain professional, she couldn't help being drawn to him.

Laura sighed. "I think I'm going to need more wine. Fiona, do you like this guy?"

"I really do," she admitted, thinking back over the last couple of days. Luke was funny and gorgeous and smart, and men like that didn't grow on trees. "That's the problem, you know? I really do like him."

"Then enjoy him. Stop overthinking everything. Just accept this for what it is and appreciate it while it lasts."

Could she do that?

"Stop thinking," Laura said as if she could see the indecision written on Fiona's face. "Just relax for once and go with it."

She wasn't the most impulsive person in the world. And she definitely wasn't the one-night-stand kind of woman. Heck, it had been nearly a year since her last date. She liked to take her time. Get to know a guy before she had sex with him. Color her old-fashioned. But her personal rules seemed to be flying out a window when it came to Luke Barrett. She was so far out of her comfort zone, she couldn't even *see* it.

Luke Barrett was the kind of man who came along once in a lifetime. Fiona thought about him. Remembered that kiss. The way he felt pressed up against her. The fire in his eyes when he looked at her.

And she knew, trouble or not, she was going to risk it.

Late the next morning, Jamison Barrett was in his study at home. Church services with Loretta were finished and the rest of the day was his. He didn't quite know what to do with himself, though. In spite of his wife's assurances, Jamison was worried. If he was losing his mind, then he needed Luke back more than ever. And if Fiona Jordan failed at her task, Jamison didn't know how he'd manage it.

"Hey, Pop."

He looked up from his desk, startled to see his oldest grandson stroll into the room. "Cole? What're you doing here?"

"What do you mean?" Cole laughed a little uncertainly and tucked one hand into the pocket of his casual slacks. "We've had this planned for a week."

"Hello, Pop." Susan came in behind Cole, carrying Oliver, a blond boy with big blue eyes like his mother's and a smile just like Cole's.

"Susan!" Jamison came around the desk and scooped Oliver into his arms. "I wasn't expecting you and this little devil."

Susan smoothed her perfect hair and gave him a curious look. "I thought we were set for brunch today after your meeting with Cole…"

Jamison felt a hot jolt that he hopefully managed to hide. Oliver slapped both hands together in excitement and shouted, "Papa!"

Grinning at his great-grandson, Jamison set the toddler onto his feet and said, "Go see Nana in the kitchen. She's always got cookies."

The boy took off like a shot and not surprisingly, Susan was right behind him. How the woman managed to run in three-inch heels was beyond Jamison, but if there was one thing you could say about his granddaughter-in-law, she was devoted to her son.

When she and the boy were gone, Jamison turned to look at Cole. "Not that I'm unhappy to see all of you…but why are you here and what's this about brunch?"

Cole just stared at him for a long minute. "We've got a meeting scheduled for today about the new Christmas line, Pop."

Jamison frowned and shook his head. "That's tomorrow."

"No," Cole said softly, carefully. "It's today. You

said you wanted to get it out of the way on Sunday so you could talk to marketing tomorrow at work."

Jamison scrubbed one hand across the back of his neck. He didn't remember saying that. Or even thinking it.

"And you said since we'd be working at the house, I should bring Susan and Oliver, and we'd do a Sunday brunch at the yacht club."

Jamison took a breath and held it. It was as if Cole were speaking Greek. He didn't remember anything about this. This didn't make sense. None of it did. A man didn't wake up one morning to find a giant hole in his metaphorical marble bag. Wasn't this something that slipped up on you? Weren't there small signs before big ones—like forgetting entire conversations?

"Are you okay, Pop?" Cole's gaze was steady and filled with the concern Jamison hated to see.

"Fine. I just forgot, is all." He was forgetting too damn much here lately, but he wasn't going to admit that to Cole. Or anyone else, for that matter—except Loretta, of course.

"You wrote it into your calendar last week."

Had he? Jamison searched his memory, but he didn't remember changing the meeting to Sunday. Worry coiled inside him like a snake. But just as quickly, he dismissed it. Damn it, he *knew* he'd set up that meeting for Monday. Irritated now, Jamison opened the calendar program on his computer. His home computer and his work unit were linked, so he could make changes or plans at either location.

Cole was the one who'd given him this program, telling Jamison that it would make his life easier. How in the hell going through a program was easier than a damn pen and paper was beyond him, but since it was a gift, Jamison had felt obligated to use it. "I know I wrote it down, boy. For tomorrow."

He scrolled through the program until he found what he was looking for and once he had, he felt worse than ever. There it was. *Sunday—Cole: Christmas line. Brunch with family.*

He swallowed back a knot of fear lodged in his throat. What the hell was happening to him? He never forgot a meeting. Hell, up until last year, he'd kept all of his appointments in his head and had never missed one.

Now he glared at the screen accusingly. As if it had somehow changed what he'd written.

"Pop?"

Cole's voice was hesitant, filled with distress, and Jamison hated it. He didn't need sympathy or concern. And he wanted it less.

"I'm fine," he insisted, in spite of the niggling doubts rattling through him. If there was a problem, he'd take care of it himself. The last thing he needed was people fluttering about him, treating him like a damn invalid—or worse. Pushing those thoughts aside, Jamison looked at his grandson and forced a smile he was nowhere near feeling.

Cole had his own wife and son to worry about. He didn't need to be thinking that his grandfather was on a slippery slope, balanced on one leg.

"Must have been too busy to notice," he said brusquely. "With Luke gone, I'm having to pick up a lot of slack in the company."

"You don't have to do it alone, Pop," Cole said stiffly. "I'm your grandson, too, you know. If you need help at the business, tell me. I can take over Luke's accounts. He's not the only one of us who grew up working at Barrett Toys and Tech."

Well, Jamison thought, he'd walked right into that one. It was a bone of contention for Cole that he wasn't stepping into Luke's shoes.

"I know that," he said, nodding. Cole was the oldest, but if truth be told, Luke was the more mature one. The one with the vision to see the company and where it could go. The fact that they were now arguing about that vision didn't matter. Cole was more about being in the moment rather than seeing the big picture, and that wasn't a trait that made for a good company president.

Still, he didn't need to get into all of that now. Looking at Cole, Jamison told himself that maybe he was being too hard on the boy. But he'd watched Luke and Cole grow up. He'd seen their personalities develop and though he loved them both, Jamison wasn't blind to their faults. Luke was always in the future, ignoring the present—and Cole was interested in a paycheck, but not the work.

"Maybe soon," Jamison hedged, "we'll have a talk about that." But if Fiona Jordan did the job he was paying her to accomplish, he wouldn't have to. Still, Cole knew nothing about that. "For right now, though, we'll go on the way we have been." He nodded and winked at Cole. "You never know, Luke might come back."

"Sure, Pop." Disappointment and frustration briefly crossed Cole's features, but an instant later, he'd buried whatever he was feeling beneath his usual smile. "We'll do it your way for now."

"That's good. So," Jamison said, sitting down at his desk again, "if you're ready, we can take care of this meeting right now."

"Okay." Cole took a seat, opened up his tablet and started talking.

Jamison listened. He really did. He even made notes when appropriate. But the back of his mind was filled with whispering voices, and none of them were comforting.

An hour later, Fiona somehow found herself on Luke's private jet, feeling like a peasant in a palace.

She was used to dragging herself through security, waiting at a crowded gate on uncomfortable chairs and then squeezing into tiny seats built for a butt a little smaller than her own.

This kind of luxury, she told herself as she looked at her surroundings, was going to make flying coach even more miserable in the future. There were two black leather sofas on either side of the sleek jet, and toward the front of the plane, a conversational group of six black leather chairs faced one another.

There were tables, reading lamps and a thick, plush white carpet on the floor. A flat-screen TV was on one wall and there were even fresh flowers in a copper vase that had been bolted to one of the tables. Slowly, she sank down onto one of the sofas and idly ran one hand across the cool, smooth surface, as if to convince herself she was really there and not dreaming.

Her gaze locked on Luke, talking with his own private flight attendant, the pilot and the copilot. She'd been introduced to all three of them when she'd come aboard and had even had a brief tour of the cockpit—an impressive and confusing wall of switches, lights and buttons.

And as distracted as she was by the plane and the luxury of not having to fight through a crowded airport, Fiona could barely take her eyes off Luke.

He wore a dark blue suit, pale blue shirt and scarlet tie. His hair, for some reason, kept capturing her attention. Too long for a businessman and too short for a surfer, and her fingers itched to touch it. His eyes were so blue, she felt as if she could drown in them. And when he turned his head to look at her, she felt a sharp jolt of electricity that set every nerve in her body sizzling.

It was that look that had kept her sleepless the night before. That *knowing* gleam in his eyes. Well, that and the memory of the kiss they'd shared in the garden. She had the distinct feeling she would remember that kiss even if she lived to be one hundred.

The feel of him pressed against her. The rush of his mouth on hers, his breath sliding into her lungs. The fire he'd kindled inside her had burned brightly all night, driving her half-crazy with an aching need that still throbbed with every beat of her heart.

Her gaze locked with his, Fiona realized she was sorry this weekend was over. It had started out as a job, but somehow it had become more than that. Now she was caught up in something completely different and she had no idea how it would end. Or where they would go from here.

When they were back in Orange County, she'd have to keep seeing him—that had been the original plan, after all. She still had to convince him to go back to the family company. But with that kiss, she had realized she wanted to keep seeing him because she simply wanted to. But sleeping with him was something else entirely. If she did and then he walked away at the end of the weekend, then she'd failed at her job. And there was still a big lie hanging between them that she really didn't want to think about. And what if he expected their weekend to end, well, with the weekend?

Too many thoughts were crashing through her mind at once and she instantly recalled Laura saying, *You always overthink everything.* Well, maybe her friend was right. Maybe it was time to stop thinking and just see what would happen.

A moment later, Luke walked toward her in long, almost lazy strides and Fiona's breath caught in her lungs. Honestly, the man was dangerous. Her heartbeat kept jumping into a fast gallop and that couldn't be healthy.

"We'll be cleared to take off in a few minutes."

"Okay." If she hadn't accepted his offer of a ride back to Southern California, right about now Fiona would have been sitting in the crowded airport waiting to be shuffled onto a jam-packed, uncomfortable plane. Not to mention, she wouldn't be with Luke. This was so much better. And so far out of her 'normal' world, she was a little off-balance. Of course, just being with Luke made her feel unsteady, so...

He helped her up, then drew her to one of the matching chairs. "We'll sit here for takeoff."

"A lot better than what I'm used to," she said, snapping her seat belt as she turned to watch him sit beside her.

He gave her a half smile that tugged at something inside her. "You can fly with me whenever you like."

"Well, that's a tempting offer," she mused, wondering if he meant it or if he was just being charming. Either way, it worked.

So strange, she thought, watching him. A few days ago, she didn't know him. Had never heard of him, really. And today, she was sitting beside him, feeling a tangle of emotions she'd never experienced before.

"I'm hoping so," he admitted, then turned to look at the woman approaching.

She was tall, wearing black slacks, a white long-sleeved blouse and a bright red scarf knotted at her neck. She was carrying two glasses of champagne and when she delivered them, she smiled. "Enjoy your flight. If you need me, Mr. Barrett, I'll be with the pilot as you requested."

"Thanks, Janice. We'll be fine."

So, he'd arranged for them to be alone. Oddly enough, that didn't make Fiona nervous at all. She took a sip of the bubbling wine and let the froth of it settle on her tongue for a moment before swallowing. Nope, not nervous. Eager, maybe.

The last few days had been so much more than she'd thought they would be. She'd gone there to do her job, but she'd never expected to be so drawn to Luke. So tempted by him. She'd never known a man who could turn her inside out so easily. Why did it have to be this man? They were separated not just by the lie that was hanging between them, but by the fact that she was in no way a part of his world. A world of private jets, for heaven's sake. No, sleeping with him would be a huge mistake.

Was it hot in the airplane, she wondered. Or was it just her?

Fiona took another sip of the cold champagne. "Oh yes. Definitely better than coach."

He grinned. "I told Janice we wouldn't be needing her after takeoff. It's only a ninety-minute flight, after all."

"Sure." Her mind was working, dancing, jumping from one thought to another. Ninety minutes could be a long time if you spent it wisely. Fly with him anytime? She doubted that would happen in the future. So why not take Laura's advice, stop thinking for a while, and just enjoy where she was and who she was with?

It wasn't like her at all to simply give in to her own wants and needs. She was more the type to think things through from every angle. Being impulsive was just counter to her nature. So why was she considering being just that?

Nerves rattled her, but Fiona tamped them down. If there were…consequences to pay, then she would pay them. Later. But if this weekend was all she would have of Luke Barrett, Fiona didn't want to waste it. For once in her life, she was going to leap without worrying about the fall. Just this once, she would take a chance. Risk it.

She felt the hum of the jet's engines as they revved, and the plane started taxiing to the runway. It felt as if she were doing the same thing. Moving inexorably forward.

"Once we're in the air," Luke said, leaning in closer to her, "I'll show you around."

She blinked at him. "There's more?"

He only smiled and then their plane was racing down the runway. Her heartbeat kept pace, thundering in her chest. Looking into his blue eyes was almost hypnotic. He could capture her with a glance. Her blood heated in her veins and she took another sip of the champagne to ease the fire. But nothing could do that.

The jet raced faster, then lifted into the air. As always, Fiona's stomach did a quick jitter, but this time, she had the feeling it was more being with Luke rather than her fear of flying.

A few minutes later, they were high above the banks of clouds she could see outside the windows. The jet's engines settled into a throaty purr that hummed in the background. Luke unhooked his seat belt, then held out a hand to her. She set her champagne aside and slipped her hand into his. He curled his fingers around hers and held on, and Fiona didn't mind in the slightest.

His skin next to hers made heat swarm through her and Fiona started a silent mantra, demanding that her hormones take a nap. They weren't listening to her, but she kept trying. Laura's advice aside, she couldn't help thinking that this connection she felt to Luke was not a good thing.

He was a job. He wasn't hers to care for or to dream about. If not for his grandfather, none of this would be happening. She still had to complete the job she'd been hired to do. What was she thinking even considering going to bed with him?

For heaven's sake, she'd known him about three days. Fiona couldn't remember a time when she'd been so willing to go with her instincts rather than planning something out. Still, it wasn't as if he was a complete stranger, was it?

A voice in the back of her mind said that the last three days, they'd been together almost nonstop. They'd talked more than most people did during weeks of getting to know each other. She liked him. A lot. And that worried her a little, because she had zero business building fantasies in her mind that centered on Luke Barrett. Just standing here, in his private jet, told her that much. They were from separate worlds. She had no place in the kind of universe he inhabited and no illusions about it, either.

Nothing in her life had prepared her for this man and she didn't think anything could have. He gave her hand a squeeze and her insides leaped into life again.

Take a nap, hormones, she thought to herself. *Take a nap*.

"And this is the bedroom," Luke said, opening a door to a room at the back of the plane.

"Handy," she answered, looking around. The room was small, but plush. A queen-size bed covered in a dark red duvet, twin tables and a television on the wall.

She looked up at him and knew there wasn't a chance in hell her hormones would be napping.

Six

His gaze was locked on her, and Fiona felt the heat of it bathing her. The power of his stare was like a touch. She could *feel* him looking at her.

"The bathroom's right here," he was saying. "Though there's another up front by the cockpit."

"Right." She laughed a little, shaking her head. This was so far from her normal life it was as if she'd landed on a different planet. "Of course. A one-bedroom, two-bath plane. Sure."

He quirked an eyebrow. "Are you okay?"

"Honestly? I don't know." She glanced around the room, taking it all in before turning her gaze back on him. Was he really so used to living like this that he didn't even see how weird it was?

"I'm fine. It's just—usually when I fly, I call it luxury if the seat next to me is empty."

He shrugged and tucked his hands into his pockets. "Yeah, I can see that."

"But you've always lived like this."

Nodding, he said only, "Pretty much."

The plane's engines hummed beneath their feet and set up a vibration that echoed in her nervous system.

"My father was a pilot, so he liked having his own plane."

"Does he still?"

Luke's features tightened. "No. He and my mom died in a plane crash."

"Oh God. I'm so sorry." She didn't know which was worse, the pain in his eyes or the matter-of-fact way he'd said it. Fiona hadn't grown up with a family, and she knew how awful that had been. The emptiness, the wish for more, for love, to be wanted. Needed. But she couldn't even imagine the pain of *having* a family and then losing them like that.

"I was a kid," he said softly. "My cousin Cole's parents were with them. They were headed to Florida on a vacation and went down halfway there. No one survived."

Fiona didn't question her instincts this time. She just went with them. Wrapping her arms around his waist, she laid her head on his chest and simply held on. There was nothing she could say. No way to help. But she could see old pain in his eyes and hear it in his voice, and it was in her nature to try to offer whatever comfort she could.

When his arms came around her and Fiona's heartbeat jumped, she knew the decision she'd just made was going to lead to more than comfort.

Luke threaded his fingers through her hair and pulled her head back. Looking down into her eyes, he shook his head as if in wonder. "You're…unsettling."

She stared up at him, gave him a small smile and said, "Thank you."

He laughed shortly. "Figures you'd see that as a compliment."

Her heart jumped into a fast rhythm. "You really do say the nicest things."

He grinned, bent his head and kissed her. Fiona's mind scrambled so fast, it was a wonder she remembered how to breathe. They were standing beside a bed. In a jet. Alone.

Sex was bound to happen. Right? She'd already decided to go for it…to surrender to whatever was happening between them. And she vowed to not regret it later.

He deepened the kiss, and Fiona eagerly matched him. Her breath was coming short and hard. Her heartbeat raced and the blood in her veins was like lava. Every square inch of her skin felt as if it were on fire.

When he lifted his head and looked down at her, Fiona could see the same reaction on his face that she felt sure was stamped on hers.

"Are we doing this?" he asked, voice deep, quiet.

"I think we really are." Fiona shut down all her doubts.

Because none of that mattered right now. The only thing she could think was that she needed to touch him and be touched. She wanted to feel him deep inside her. She needed Luke Barrett in a way she'd never needed before.

And today, she was going to surrender to her own needs. This wasn't about anything but the current sizzling between her and Luke and Fiona wanted more than anything to indulge herself in him. Whatever came next…she'd worry about that when she had to.

A half smile curved one side of his mouth. "Really glad to hear that."

Then he kissed her again, and Fiona stopped thinking altogether. With his mouth on hers, his tongue stroking against hers, all she could do was *feel*. And there was so much, it was as if her brain were short-circuiting and she didn't miss it at all.

He tore his mouth from hers, tugged the hem of her red-and-white-striped boatneck shirt up and over her head, then tossed it aside. The cool air touched her skin and only enflamed it further. He stared at her black lace bra and sighed before flipping open the catch in front. Then his hands cupped her breasts and Fiona groaned.

His thumbs and forefingers tugged and pulled at her nipples, and she felt it all the way to her core.

She was hot, achy and filled with so many needs she couldn't have named them all even if she could have spoken. Which she couldn't.

"I've wanted to touch you since that first day," he murmured, bending down to kiss her again. It was a hard, fast, desperate kiss that Fiona missed the moment it ended.

"Yes," she finally said, when she could gather enough coherent thought to form a sentence. "I remember how 'happy' you were when we first met."

He grinned. "You're about to find out that I'm a hell of a lot 'happier' right now."

"Promises, promises," she muttered as his hands dropped to the hem of her short black skirt. She'd always loved that skirt. Today, she thought it just might be her favorite piece of clothing.

Because it gave him quick, easy access to the one part of her body that was screaming for attention.

In seconds, his talented fingers had found the strip of elastic at her black panties and sent them sliding down her legs so she could kick them off. Then he cupped her with one hand and she instantly began rocking into his touch. She couldn't stop herself. Didn't want to stop. What she wanted was what he was giving her. A ride into oblivion. Release. And that thought alone kept her standing, moving into him.

One finger, then two, moved within her, stroking, caressing. His thumb found her center and rubbed that one, so sensitive bud until her eyes were wheeling in her head and breathing became an extreme sport.

If she had stood outside herself, she might have been embarrassed to be mostly naked, with a fully dressed man who was sliding his fingers inside her. But she wouldn't have changed anything.

Fiona felt as if she'd been primed for an orgasm from the moment she'd landed on his lap. So, it was no surprise when her body was suddenly on the broken verge of shattering.

Until he stopped.

Fiona blinked and stared up at him. "What? Why?"

"Nope," he said flatly. "You're not going there without me."

She watched him tear his clothes off, tossing his elegant suit to one side until he was naked and, she saw...*impressive*.

He unzipped her skirt and let it fall, then he tumbled her back onto the wide bed behind her and followed her down.

His hands claimed her body while his mouth took hers. Their tongues twisted and tangled together, breath sliding from one to the other of them. Fiona clutched at his shoulders and slid her fingertips down his muscular arms, loving the feel of him. The heat in his body that speared into hers.

She kissed him with everything she had and threw one leg over his hip, pulling that erection closer, closer. When the tip of him rubbed over her, she groaned and broke their kiss long enough to mutter, "For heaven's sake, do it. Do it now."

He reached to the closest table, opened the drawer and pulled out a condom.

"Handy," she murmured.

"I try," he countered.

In a blink, he had sheathed himself, and then he was kneeling between her thighs, holding her body open to his gaze. Fiona squirmed with impatience.

"I feel like we've been doing the whole foreplay thing for days," she whispered, looking up, into his summer-blue eyes. "Can we go for the big show now?"

He grinned. "Have I mentioned I really like your attitude?"

"Nope, but you can. Later."

"Right." He pushed into her body with one long, hard stroke.

She groaned. Fiona's head went back into the mattress and she stared blindly at the jet's ceiling as she adjusted to his size. He filled her completely, and she didn't know how she'd lived so long without having him inside her.

Then he rocked his hips against her, and everything got even better. A delicious friction built up between them as he moved inside her. He set a rhythm that she raced to keep up with. Her body was humming, her mind shutting down. She fought for breath, hoped her heart wouldn't explode and rocked her hips with his every movement. "More," she groaned. "More."

"Yes," he ground out. "Always more."

She was so close. So near the teetering edge of oblivion Fiona could almost taste it. Then he changed things up and threw her for a loop.

He sat back on his heels, drawing her up with him until she was straddling him. Eye to eye, they looked at each other, gazes locked as Fiona took charge of the rhythm. The pace. She moved on him, taking him deeper and deeper inside her and still it wasn't enough. She swiveled her hips against him, creating a new kind of friction that drove them both to the brink.

"You're amazing," he muttered, leaning in to take her mouth with his.

She licked her lips when the kiss was over, as if she could draw the taste of him into her.

His hands locked on her hips, guiding her, pushing her, helping her keep that wild, frantic rhythm at a breathless pace, because they were now caught together in a net of desperation. When the first splintering sensation jolted her, Fiona grabbed hold of him and kept moving, kept pushing herself higher and faster, riding that incredible pulse of pleasure that rocked her right to the bone.

While she shattered in his arms, she felt his release shake through him. His grip on her tightened; he clenched his jaw and kept his gaze fixed on her as if seeing her fed what he was feeling.

And when the crash was over, they fell to the bed, still locked together.

* * *

"Nice to keep a supply of condoms in the drawer," she murmured.

Luke grinned. "Yeah. I bought some this morning. Just in case."

She turned her head to look at him and Luke thought her eyes looked darker, deeper, somehow. Almost as if they were pulling him in. "So you thought I was a sure thing?"

"I hoped," he admitted, leaning in to get another kiss. God, the taste of her pumped through him with a life of its own. He'd just had her and he wanted her again. More than before because now he knew just how good it was.

"Good call," she said, and gave a lovely, long sigh. "That was…"

"Yeah. If we're this good in the air, imagine how good we'll be on the ground."

Her gaze snapped to his. "Will we?"

He smoothed her hair back, indulging himself by sliding his fingers through that soft, dark brown silk. "I'm not finished yet. You?"

She dragged her fingertips along his chest, and he sucked in a gulp of air. "No, I'm not finished, either."

"Like I said before. I like your attitude." He leaned over her and took one of her nipples into his mouth. He smiled against her at the quick catch of her breath. His tongue and teeth worked that dark pink bud until she was writhing beneath him and all Luke could think was how glad he was he'd bought the large box of condoms.

Then he lost himself in her again and stopped thinking entirely.

An hour later, Luke hooked one arm behind his head and said, "We'll be landing soon."

"Back to the real world."

"This isn't real?" he asked, turning his head to look at her. She was beautiful. Her eyes alone were enough to spellbind a man. And the minute that thought hit, he scowled to himself. Luke wouldn't allow that. In his world, the plan ruled all. And Fiona was definitely not a part of the plan. He wasn't spellbound and wasn't about to be, either. But he could appreciate a beautiful woman he'd just had the most incredible sex of his life with.

She grinned and he worried again. "This isn't *my* reality," she said. "It's a great place to visit, don't get me wrong. But when I get home, I've got to pay bills, answer emails and do some laundry. *That* is reality."

"I pay bills and do emails," he pointed out.

"And the laundry?"

He shrugged. "The housekeeper does it."

She laughed, and he liked the sound of it in spite of the fact that she was laughing at *him*.

"Of course she does."

Still frowning, he changed the subject, since he was suddenly *embarrassed* about having a house-keeper. If she found out he had a cook, too, she might laugh herself sick.

"Why don't you let me take you to dinner tomorrow night?"

"Really?" she seemed surprised, and frankly, so was he.

When they'd first boarded this plane, Luke hadn't planned on seeing her again once they got home. He wasn't interested in a relationship—he had way too much going on at the moment. But he didn't care for the thought of letting her go, either. Now, after that bout of incredible sex, he was even more interested in sticking around for a while. He didn't want to consider why. Refused to think of what that might mean. He wouldn't be distracted by emotional entanglements. This wasn't about emotion anyway. This was simple, beautiful lust, and he would stay with her until the desire for her had ebbed.

"Why not?"

"Well, for one thing, I've got a job tomorrow evening."

"Doing what?"

She studied him for a long second or two, then said, "Why don't you come over and you can go with me to my appointment? Then we can have dinner after."

Go with her. On what? A treasure hunt like she'd had the day before when she dug through wet towels to find a stuffed alligator? But even as he thought it, he realized he didn't care. "All right. It's a date."

"Great." She leaned over to kiss him, then smiled. "I'm just going to put my clothes on. Your flight attendant might guess what we were up to, but I'd rather she didn't see me naked."

He watched her snatch up her clothes and step into the attached bathroom. Luke wasn't sure why he'd agreed to go along on her job. He'd thought a nice dinner and then another great bout of lovemaking.

What had he gotten himself into here? And why didn't he care?

Late the next afternoon, Fiona and Laura sat in matching lawn chairs watching Travis chase a bright red ball across the lawn. The little boy's laughter spilled from him and floated behind him like soap bubbles on the air.

"So, he's coming over," Laura said.

"Yep."

"To go on your job with you."

"Yep."

"Okay, my question is, *why*?"

Fiona had wondered that, too. She'd thought it was going to be hard to stay close enough to him to complete her job for his grandfather. Instead, Luke himself had suggested meeting again. Was it the sex? Because it had been really great, but sex wasn't *everything*. "Because I'm irresistible?"

Laura laughed. "That must be it."

Fiona grinned. She looked at Travis, a two-year-old whose only problem at the moment was catching up to his favorite ball. Maybe Laura right. Maybe she did overthink everything. Maybe she should take a clue from Travis and just focus on what was in front of her in the moment.

A soft wind swept over them and nodded the heads of the gem-colored pansies in Laura's flower bed. At the duplex next door, the Gonzalez girls sat on the porch, each of them playing on her own tablet. They, too, were focused on the moment. So the trick was to focus on what was *important* right now.

"I don't know why he wanted to see me again, but I couldn't say no. Not only is he gorgeous and funny and smart and *way* talented in bed, he's my job, too." She winced. "I can't believe I had sex with him."

"On a plane." Laura sighed and looked wistful. "I'm so jealous."

Fiona looked back at the Gonzalez kids again. They didn't talk to each other or laugh together or anything. They could have been twin statues for all the interaction happening between them. She sighed and shook her head.

Funny that she'd never noticed how many kids were glued to tablets before working for Jamison Barrett. The girls on that porch were ten and eight. Too young to be that wrapped up in a computer.

Frowning, Fiona made a mental note to point the girls out to Luke and to remember that he wasn't her "date." He was her job.

"This is crazy," she muttered. "*I'm* crazy."

"Yeah, probably," Laura mused. "But, Fiona, you never do anything wild or outrageous. Honey, you never take something for yourself. So maybe you were due."

She had a point, as much as Fiona hated to admit it. But that didn't let her off the hook, did it? Was doing something for herself enough of a reason to be with Luke? Was that fair to him? And what happened when he inevitably discovered the truth about their first meeting? She was lying to Luke about who she was and how she'd met him. He thought it was all an accident of fate. What would he say if he found out his grandfather had paid her to be there? Had arranged for her plane ticket and hotel room just so that she could convince him to come back to the company?

Wincing, she silently admitted she knew just what he'd say. *Goodbye.* So she had to remember that whatever was between them, it was temporary. An anomaly to her daily life. No more permanent than a sunset…beautiful, but quickly gone.

"Oh my… You know I love my honey," Laura whispered beside her. "But damn, Fiona…"

She didn't have to look to know that Luke had arrived. Laura's glassy-eyed stare was enough to alert her to his presence. Fiona was pretty sure she'd had the same expression on her face the first time she saw him. Still, she turned her head to watch the man approach.

He was wearing a suit again. Of course. She idly wondered if he even owned a pair of jeans. The suit was black with faint gray pinstripes. He wore a white dress shirt with a dark gray tie, and his too-long hair was ruffling in the sea breeze.

It was late afternoon, so the neighborhood kids were home from school. Somewhere down the street, a basketball thumped like the heartbeat of the neighborhood. Skateboard wheels growled across the sidewalks, and the sounds made her smile. At least *some* kids were outside and not staring at a screen.

"Hi!" Fiona stood up and walked to him, suddenly feeling very underdressed. Her beige ankle pants, yellow long-sleeved shirt and taupe Skechers really didn't hold up against that suit.

He slipped one hand to the back of her neck and leaned in to claim a quick, hard kiss. A zip of something amazing shot through Fiona like a whipcrack. A job, she thought frantically. He was a job. But even reminding herself of that fact didn't change what she was willing to risk just to be with him.

"I've been wanting to do that all day," he admitted.

A job and so much more.

"Well, don't be shy," she said. "Do it again."

He grinned and took advantage of the invitation.

Her head was spinning even as she gave herself a mental talking-to. Hadn't she just decided that she had to remain professional? Why was it that her best intentions flew out the window the minute she was close to him?

When she came up for air, Laura was standing right beside her. Her best friend was five inches shorter than Fiona's five nine, and her body was substantially curvier. Her wide smile was friendly, and her blue eyes were sparkling with interest and curiosity.

"Hi, I'm Laura. Best friend. Neighbor. Landlord." She held out one hand and Luke shook it.

"Nice to meet you," he said. "Luke Barrett."

"Fee!" Travis came racing up, grabbed hold of Fiona's legs and turned his face to her. "Up, Fee!"

"Right." She lifted him, sat him on her hip and said, "Luke, this is my boyfriend, Travis. He's the jealous type, so watch your step."

"I'll keep it in mind. He looks pretty tough."

"Oh, he is. Able to destroy a living room in less than ten minutes," Laura put in and scooped her son from Fiona.

"Maybe he could use something to keep him so busy learning he wouldn't have time for destruction," Luke said.

Now it was Fiona's turn to frown. Just the thought of this active little boy sitting in front of a computer tablet when he could be running in circles refocused her on the job at hand.

Fiona tugged at Luke's arm and pointed him at the house next door. The two girls were still there. Still staring at their screens. Still so absorbed with their tablets it was as if they'd forgotten they weren't alone.

"Busy like them, you mean?" Fiona asked. "That's Elena and Teresa Gonzalez. I'd introduce you, but they're zoned out. Being *busy.*"

Luke looked at the girls and frowned thoughtfully. Fiona thought that maybe she'd scored a point. But whatever he was thinking, he didn't say. He simply shifted his gaze to her. "You ready to leave?"

Fiona let it go. For now. But she'd be talking to him about the girls and their technology again later. "Sure. Let me get my purse. I'll see you tomorrow, Laura."

"Have fun," her friend said, and headed off to get Travis's ball.

Luke followed her inside and stood practically at attention in her small living room. He looked around and she wished she knew what he was thinking. Fiona had no idea where he lived, but she knew that wherever it was, his place was nothing like hers.

Fiona's living room was painted a deep maroon and she'd installed the white crown molding herself. Her windows didn't have curtains because Fiona hated them, but she had installed window shades that she pulled down at night for a little privacy. There was a green love seat and two club chairs covered in a fabric that boasted wild sprays of flowers, and a coffee table she'd found in a thrift shop. She'd sanded and painted the table a pale yellow, adding to the garden feel of the room.

"It's a nice place."

"Thanks." Her entire apartment was probably the size of his closet, but she loved the home she'd built for herself. Every room was a different color, and she'd filled the apartment with furniture she loved.

So every time she walked into her apartment, Fiona felt satisfaction and a sense of…rightness she'd never known as a kid.

She reached over and turned on one of a pair of dented brass lamps she'd found at an auction, and soft light spilled into the room. "I just need to get my purse." She stopped and looked at him. "You don't have to wear a tie, you know. You could… loosen up a little."

He smoothed one hand down the gray tie and said, "I came straight from work. And my gray tie is my loose tie."

She grinned at the spark of humor in his eyes. He really was the whole package. Smart. Funny. And so sexy it took her breath away. "Is that right?"

"Oh yeah." He nodded solemnly. "Red ties? Power. Navy? All business. Gray? Casual and loose."

"Wow, I didn't know they made a tie for 'casual.'"

"Now you do." He checked his watch. "What time is your appointment?"

"Twenty minutes or so. But he's in Seal Beach. It won't take long to get there."

"He?" Luke lifted one eyebrow. "What're you doing for 'him'?"

"It's a secret." Fiona smiled, grabbed her purse and headed for the door. "Let's go."

Seven

Whatever Luke had been expecting, this wasn't it. The "him" in question was seventeen, extremely tall and gangly, with a hank of hair that kept falling over his eyes, and he was going to his first prom in a few weeks. He needed to know how to dance.

"Ow!" Fiona hopped a little after the boy stepped on her foot for the third time.

Luke winced. This was painful to watch. How the hell did Fiona make a living doing all of these short-term jobs? Teaching a kid to dance. Finding an alligator. Now she'd probably be limping for a week.

"I'm never getting this."

"You're doing fine, Kenny," she said to the boy, who towered over her. "You just have to relax."

"How can I relax when I'm worried about stepping on you? I can't do this. I'll break Amber's foot." He shook his head and held both hands up. "I'll just stick to the fast dances."

Luke sighed and shook his head. He'd been watching this disaster for a half hour now, and he had to wonder how this kid was the star of the basketball team. He had zero rhythm. He was too tense, too. He held on to Fiona like she was a live grenade about to explode. He was probably more relaxed on the court, Luke thought. Hell, he'd have to be.

"Okay." He stood up and walked to Fiona. "Let's try something else." Talking to Kenny, he said, "You just sit down and watch." To Fiona, he added, "We'll show him how to do it."

How he'd gotten into this, he wasn't sure. Luke had thought about Fiona all day. What he'd wanted was to get her alone on a flat surface somewhere. Instead, he was slow dancing for a teenager in his parents' den.

"Oh, good idea," she said, and gave Kenny an encouraging smile. "Watch us for a minute or two, then we'll try again."

"It's useless." He swung his dark brown hair out of his eyes and scowled.

"Only if you quit," Luke said. Taking Fiona in his arms, he looked into her eyes, but his words were for Kenny. "Hold her closer."

"I can't hold on to Fiona like that. It's too weird, man."

"You're practicing," Luke reminded him. "You'll want to hold Amber close, right?"

"Well, yeah…"

"Okay. Hold her close." He pulled Fiona in tightly to him. "Put your feet in place before the music starts—on either side of one of her feet."

Kenny studied him. "Okay…"

"You don't have to be fancy about it. Going in circles will get the job done for you." Luke started moving and paid no attention to Fiona's bright smile. She was enjoying this. Well, surprisingly enough, so was he.

The music played and Luke moved with it. "Listen to the beat and keep up with it. Slow or fast, if you stay with the beat you won't look uncoordinated."

"Hey!" Kenny the basketball star was offended.

"And you'll notice, I'm not stepping on her feet because I'm barely lifting mine."

"Yeah. That works…" Kenny nodded and looked a little less defeated.

"Her steps will follow yours in the dance. It's just instinct. You act like you know what you're doing, and it'll be fine." Of course, teenage hormones would be soaring. And he knew that because holding on to Fiona like this with the slow music streaming from the speakers on the wall made him want to pick her up and carry her out to the car.

Which meant, he told himself, lesson over. Luke stepped back and motioned to Kenny. "You try it now."

Fiona grinned at him, then gave Kenny an encouraging smile. "You can do this. And you'll be glad you did."

Kenny shrugged. "It's your feet."

"I'll risk it."

Luke stood aside and watched as Kenny did just as he'd been told. Fiona smiled up at the boy and, as the music played and they began to dance, Kenny visibly relaxed. It wasn't exactly an old Gene Kelly movie, but it was good enough for prom, and now the kid knew he could dance with his girlfriend without permanently maiming her.

The song ended and Kenny dropped Fiona like she was on fire. "That was awesome." He grinned and flashed a look at Luke. "Thanks, man. That works."

"You did fine."

Fiona asked, "Do you want to try it again? Just to make sure you've got it?"

"Don't have to. What he said made sense and now I know I can do it. Just plant my feet before the music."

"Excellent," Luke said.

"Okay, then." Fiona reached up and gave the kid a hug. "Lesson over. Have a great time at the dance, Kenny."

"I will now. Thanks." He jerked his hair out of his eyes and looked at Luke again. "Thanks. Really."

"You're welcome." He held out a hand and the kid shook it with a hard grip. "Have fun."

After Fiona collected a check from Kenny's grateful mother, they were outside on the front walk.

Streetlights were on, casting pale white glows into the darkness. A crisp sea breeze kicked up and Fiona shivered. Automatically, he dropped one arm around her shoulders and pulled her in close.

"That was nice," she said. "What you did for Kenny."

"It was more for Amber. And you." He snorted. "I couldn't take it anymore. If I hadn't stepped in, you would have ended the night in a cast."

"It wasn't that bad." She laughed, though, and he liked the sound. "It's hard to teach a guy the guy's moves, so thanks for helping out."

"You're welcome." He looked down at her and felt his body stir again. Hell, since the moment he'd met this woman, his body had been like stone. "Not hard to sway back and forth and move in a circle."

She grinned at him. "It meant a lot to Kenny."

"Uh-huh." He couldn't have cared less about Kenny and his plans for a night of dancing and who the hell knew what else. What he'd done, he'd done for Fiona. To see that smile he was currently basking in.

He didn't like knowing that she was becoming more important to him than he cared to acknowledge. But even if his mind shied away from that thought, his body had no trouble admitting it.

"So?" she asked, and Luke was ready for any suggestion that would get them alone and naked. "Dinner. How about a burger?"

Her eyes sparkled and her lips were curved in that

smile that drove him crazy. Not the idea he'd had in mind, but it'd do. For now.

The next morning, Fiona called Jamison Barrett on the direct number he'd given her. She had to report in on her weekend with Luke. Of course, she has no intention of telling the older man about what had happened on the plane. Or last night in her apartment, for that matter. She shivered a little at the images flooding her mind and knew she'd never be able to sleep in that bed again without Luke's memory joining her.

Jamison answered and Fiona jumped.

"Yes?" He sounded distracted. Maybe that was a good thing.

"Mr. Barrett," Fiona said, rising to walk across her living room. "This is Fiona Jordan."

"Hmm? Oh. Yes. Yes. Fiona. Hello."

Frowning, she stared out at the sun-washed street. "I just wanted you to know that the weekend with Luke went very well, and I think I'm making headway."

"That's good."

His voice sounded odd to her. Less confident. The last time she spoke to him, Jamison had been brisk, impatient. Now it seemed as if he wasn't even interested in what was happening with Luke. Was he having second thoughts? Was he sorry he'd hired her in the first place?

Because Fiona could completely understand regrets. She regretted ever lying to Luke. But she couldn't be sorry she'd taken this job, because if she hadn't, she never would have met him, and she couldn't even imagine not knowing him.

How did this whole situation get so confused and tangled up? Luke loved his grandfather but couldn't work with him. Jamison loved his grandson but couldn't compromise. And Fiona? Fiona was in the middle, unsure which way to turn.

Still, she tried. "I'm seeing him again today and—"

"Right. You just get it done and we'll talk then. All right? Thank you."

He hung up and Fiona took the phone from her ear to stare at it. For a man who was so determined to win his grandson back, he seemed decidedly uninterested in hearing the report he had asked for. What was going on?

When Jamison hung up, Fiona went straight out of his mind. He had bigger problems at the moment. He stared at the contract in front of him and felt panic clawing at the edges of his soul.

His signature was on the bottom line, but damned if he remembered signing it. "Why the hell would I order skateboards from a new company when I've already got Salem's boards?"

Didn't make sense. But then, lately nothing was making sense, and Jamison felt a fresh stir of fear. And he didn't like that, either. He'd faced a lot in his lifetime. He lost his father in a world war, the loss of his sons. He'd fought his way through bad times before and he would this time, too.

He knew Cole was worried about him. And it wouldn't be long before he saw the same look of concern on Loretta's face, too. Jamison didn't think he could stand that. Maybe it was time to talk to his doctor. Get to the bottom of this. Bill Tucker was a no-nonsense kind of man. He'd be straight with Jamison. And maybe, he admitted silently, that was why he hadn't gone to see him yet. He was afraid of what Bill might have to say.

Loretta claimed it was nothing, but he couldn't help worrying. He'd seen friends diagnosed with dementia. He'd watched them slowly fade away until there was nothing of them left, and it terrified him to believe that might be happening to him.

"Pop?" Cole poked his head in the door.

"Yes." He looked up. "What is it?"

"I wanted to ask you about the order for basketballs you canceled."

"What? I didn't cancel an order." Did he?

Cole stepped into the room and his features were twisted into a mask of worry that ate at Jamison's insides. "I just got a call from Adam Carey, and he says he got the cancellation late last night."

"Last night?" Shaking his head, Jamison jumped to his feet. That should be proof that he wasn't doing this. That he hadn't lost his mind. "I was out with your grandmother last night. We went to the club for dinner..."

Cole winced and handed out the email he'd printed out. "Adam forwarded the email to me, Pop. It's definitely from you. Went out about ten last night."

Jamison studied it and an icy ball dropped into the pit of his stomach. It was from his email address. Canceling an order. But he didn't do it. Crumpling the paper in his fist, he looked at Cole. "I didn't send this."

"Pop…" Cole scrubbed one hand across his neck and looked as if he wished he were anywhere else.

Jamison knew the feeling.

"Damn it, boy, stop looking at me like I'm dying."

"I don't like this, Pop."

"Well, neither do I. Look, I don't know what's going on here, but I didn't send this." He tossed the offensive wad of paper into the trash, then sat down behind his desk again. "I'll call Adam. Set things straight."

"Good luck. He's pretty pissed."

"I said I'll take care of it." He looked back at the file on his desk, silently dismissing Cole. But his grandson didn't leave.

"Pop, do you think maybe we should talk to a doctor?"

"We?" Jamison speared his grandson with a steely look. Damned if he'd be treated like a slobbering old fool. "You having a problem you didn't tell me about?"

Cole took a breath. "Fine. You, then. Pop, you seem to be having some trouble lately, and I want you to know that I'm here." The younger man moved closer, leaned both hands on the edge of the desk and said, "I can take over for you. Handle things while you take a break. Maybe you just need a long rest."

If what he was hearing was simple familial concern, then Jamison should have been touched. But he knew that there was nothing Cole would like better than stepping into the CEO job. He'd been angling for it for years.

"How long a break, Cole? Forever?" Jamison loved his grandson, but he knew Cole's ambitions far exceeded his talents.

"You know, I'm not saying that." He pushed up from the desk. "But with Luke gone, I'm the one you can trust to take over. Pop, I'm here. Use me."

Irritation rushed in and was swamped by regret for thinking badly of Cole. Sure, he had a lot of ambition, but so had Jamison at his age. It wasn't Cole's fault now that his grandfather's brain was taking a vacation. "I know that. And I appreciate it. But I'm not ready to quit. And we don't know that Luke's gone for good, either."

Cole pushed one hand through his hair in frustration. "Luke isn't your only grandson, Pop. He isn't the only Barrett who's worked at the company since he was a kid. He's not the only man who could run this company."

There was a lot of bitterness there. More than he'd suspected.

"You're getting worked up for nothing, Cole."

Jamison shook his head and tried to understand that Cole's jealousy of his cousin was probably Jamison's fault. He'd always favored Luke because he'd seen himself in the boy. He knew that Luke was the one to run this company into the next generation. Cole was good at what he did, but he wasn't qualified to be the CEO.

It was never easy to admit unpleasant truths, but Jamison had faced it years ago. Cole, though, would never accept his own limits. Then again, maybe he shouldn't. If a person started putting limitations on what he thought he could do, then he'd never do anything.

"Am I?" Cole threw both hands up in complete exasperation. "I'm tired of being overlooked in favor of the man who left the company. Luke left. He walked out on you, Pop, and you *still* prefer him? I'm *here*. I stayed. I'm the one who gives a damn about the company. And you."

"I know." Jamison forced a smile. Truth be told, he wasn't up for a conflict right now. There were too many worries riding his possibly failing brain. Plus, he was already at war with one grandson. Did he really want another one?

"You're a good man, Cole," he said, hoping to placate him. "And I know you'll be there for me if I need you to step in. I just don't need it yet."

Clearly still irritated, Cole said, "You sure about that? You're losing it, Pop, and we both know it."

"No," he said flatly. He wasn't about to share his

worries with Cole and get the man even more worked up than he already was. "We don't. Now I've got work to do and I'm sure you do, too."

"Fine." Cole shook his head and blew out a breath. "Call Adam. Straighten it out. I'm meeting Susan and Oliver at the yacht club for lunch. I'll probably just go home from there."

Jamison nodded, unsurprised. But he couldn't help thinking, *there,* Cole. That's why you're not the one. You leave in the middle of the day. Nearly every damn day. Jamison was all for spending time with your family, but there were responsibilities to be taken care of as well. Cole ran himself ragged trying to make Susan happy and paid little if any attention to the business that's keeping them both living in their mansion in Dana Point.

Cole stormed out, and Jamison rubbed his aching temples. If Luke didn't come back, he didn't think the company would survive. Hell, at this point, he wasn't sure *he* would survive.

And on that happy thought, he picked up the phone, dialed a number and said, "Adam? Jamison Barrett here. What's all this nonsense about a canceled order?"

Fiona loved the beach in winter. The sand was empty but for a few die-hard souls and the waves only called to the most dedicated surfers. In February, the sea looked slate gray and the wind that blew past them was sharp and icy. The waves crashed on the shore, then slid back where they'd come from in lacy patterns they left behind on the wet sand.

She tipped her face into the wind and smiled. The only thing better than taking a winter walk on the beach was having Luke with her.

"I can't believe this is your view. Every day." She took a deep breath, drawing the damp sea air deep inside her. Holding her hair down, she looked up at him. "If I lived here, I'd be down on the beach every chance I got."

"Don't have many chances." He tucked a piece of her hair behind her ear and trailed his fingers down her cheek. Fiona shivered at his touch and wondered if she always would.

"Work keeps me busy," he added with a shrug.

"And your phone..." Her tone was teasing, but her words weren't.

He scowled at her. "I left it back at the house, didn't I?"

"And is not having it driving you crazy?"

"No. *You* are."

She smiled. "There you go, saying nice things again."

"I don't know what it is about you, Fiona." His gaze moved over her features before settling on her eyes. "When I'm with you I have to touch you. When I'm not with you, I'm thinking about you."

"I feel the same way," she said softly.

He pulled her into his arms and Fiona went willingly. Being with him now was worth the price she would eventually have to pay. Reaching up, she cupped his cheeks in her palms and told herself that later on, she wouldn't regret this time with him. If memories were all she was going to have, then she wanted a lot of them burned into her mind so that she'd never forget a moment of the time spent with Luke. She'd never taken something for herself. Not like this. And when this time with Luke was over, she might never feel like this again.

He turned his face into her palm and kissed it, sending pearls of heat tumbling through her. Fiona was in such deep trouble, and she didn't care. What she felt for Luke was so unexpected, such a gift, she couldn't turn away from it.

"How about we go back to my house?"

They'd stopped at his house for a drink after seeing a movie she couldn't even remember. And now all she could think was, she wanted to be inside, where people couldn't see them. Inside, where she could touch him and be touched.

"That sounds good," she said, and turned with him to walk back across the sand.

At night, his home shone like a jewel. It was right on the beach and built as if it belonged in Spain. The arched windows, the red-tiled entrance, and the trailing vines and flowers that swept across the second story all spoke of sun-drenched days and long, warm nights.

"I love your house."

"I did, too."

"Did?" She turned her face up to his.

"Yeah, I'm moving," he said. "To a cliff view where thousands of beachgoers aren't in my front yard every summer."

He had a point. The beach in winter was secluded, quiet. But the same spot in summer would be noisy and crowded and—still beautiful. "I suppose I can understand that, but I would miss the beach…"

He pulled her in close, one arm around her shoulders. "At the new house, there's a path down to the sand. And the house is close to my grandparents. They're getting older and—"

She stopped, drawing him to a stop, too. "You won't work for your grandfather, but you'll move to live closer to him?"

He stepped back and shoved both hands into his pockets—he did own a pair of jeans and looked spectacular in them. Squinting into the wind, he said, "Just because I left the company doesn't mean I left the family."

Why couldn't he see that his grandfather was convinced that that was exactly what it meant? To Jamison Barrett, the toy company was an extension of the family. Having Luke walk away from it made Jamison feel he was leaving *them* behind as well.

"So why do you insist on staying away from the company? That *is* your family, isn't it? Why not just work through your problems with your grandfather?" Fiona looked at this conversation as an opportunity she had to take advantage of. "Like you said, they're getting older. Why not compromise?"

He seemed to think about it for a long moment before answering. The wind ruffled his hair; moonlight glittered in his eyes when he met her gaze. "Because I've got to prove this to Pop. And maybe," he said, "to myself, too. I'm right about the technological future."

"But it's Barrett Toys and *Tech*. Isn't he already compromising with you?"

"No." His features went hard and closed. "It's compromise on his terms. He'll toss me a bone, but we'd still be doing things his way. He wants to dial the tech back while I believe it should be expanded." He looked at the churning sea and talked almost to himself. "Kids today are hungry for more and more tech. Why wouldn't we want to get in on giving it to them?"

"Oh, Luke. Just because a kid wants something doesn't mean they should have it."

He whipped his head back to look into her eyes. Surprise etched on his face, he asked, "You're on his side in this?"

"I'm on nobody's side," she assured him, holding up both hands in a peace offering.

"Thanks," he muttered.

She wanted to sigh. Any other time, she'd be happy to be on his side. But in this case, Fiona thought his grandfather had a point. "I'm just saying that because something is new and shiny doesn't make it better. Like you said yourself, technology isn't going away. It's the future. Why do kids have to learn it when they should be out playing baseball or surfing or whatever?"

"Because tech is part of the society that they're growing up in. Adapting young means they'll be more flexible when tech keeps changing," he argued.

A couple holding hands walked past them but neither of them noticed. Fiona couldn't look away from Luke's eyes. This was her chance to talk to him about the rift between him and his grandfather. Yes, it was her job to convince him, but more than that, she knew what it was like to not have a family. She didn't want to watch him throw away what she'd never had.

"Did you know," she asked quietly, "that doctors are actually seeing cases of severe language delays due to screens?"

That statement caught him off guard. "What?"

Fiona had done a lot of reading on this subject, and there were studies that supported both Luke's and his grandfather's opinions. But if you were dealing with the *chance* of doing permanent harm to a child's mind, wouldn't you take the more careful route?

"You said it yourself, there are a lot of studies— good and bad—being done. Well," she said, "I saw an article about it, and I thought it sounded weird, so I read it. Apparently, small children who spend many hours a day on screens—phones, tablets—

don't develop normal language skills. Their brains are being rewired."

Luke frowned and shook his head. Bracing his feet wide apart, he folded his arms across his chest and shook his head. "I can point you to studies that say the exact opposite."

"I guess," Fiona said. "But it's scary to think about, right? This article said some toddlers have had to seek speech therapy to make up their delays. And teenagers are spending eight to twelve hours a *day* online."

His frown deepened and she wouldn't have thought that possible. "Anything can be bad if overdone."

"True." Fiona laid one hand on his forearm. "But see, that's the thing. They're kids. They're going to overdo. And according to this article, most parents are unaware of the negative consequences for their kids spending so much time on screens."

His stance relaxed a bit, but his eyes narrowed on her in suspicion. "Fiona, what are you up to?"

Slow it down, she told herself. Shaking her head, she said, "Nothing. Honestly. It's just that we've been talking about this since we met, and I decided to research it. Some kids are being digitally distracted from the real world."

"And you think that's what I'm doing?"

"Not deliberately, of course not."

The wind slapped at them both, whipping her hair across her eyes, and she pushed it free. Luke stood in front of her like a glowering giant, readying for battle. "We're selling screens. Tablets. We're not even trying to get into the video game market."

"But you sell reading games and swirling color games for toddlers," she argued. "Isn't that priming them to want to play as much as they can, and to want more involved games later?"

"Maybe." That glowering frown deepened. "I hadn't considered it, but I guess there is a case to be made for what you're saying."

"Luke, why don't you talk to your grandfather about all of this? I'm trying to see both sides and maybe your grandfather is feeling that his company is about family. And that you're walking away not just from the business, but from him. You never know. He might be more willing to compromise now that you've been gone for a while."

"No. Pop knows I love him. This isn't about that." He snorted and started walking toward the house again. "I'm willing to give on a couple of points you made. And I'm going to look into the research more deeply. But when it comes to my grandfather, you're wrong, Fiona. You don't know him like I do."

Fiona had to hurry her steps to keep up with him. Had she pushed too hard, too fast?

"People change, Luke."

"Not him, Fiona." His voice was low and almost lost in the driving wind and the throaty roar of the ocean. "I'm not saying you're completely wrong."

That was something, she told herself, so she gave him more to think about. "That article I read, it had a lot of really interesting points. The doctor wrote that screens are bad for kids, because they *need* to communicate face-to-face with other people. That it's essential for their social and emotional development."

He stopped right outside his home's enclosed patio. Plexiglass panels lifted off what looked like adobe but was probably stucco walls, to allow the view while protecting people on the patio from the fierce wind. There were chairs and tables and even a pizza oven tucked into one corner of the patio. But at the moment, all Fiona could see was Luke.

He tipped his head to one side and stared at her. "Did you *memorize* this article?"

She winced. "Sounds like it, doesn't it?"

"Sounds like you're trying to convince me that my grandfather's right."

Fiona stepped in close to him and laid one hand on his chest. "In a way, I guess I am."

He curled his hand around hers and held on. The faint wash of lights from his house fell across them. From somewhere nearby, a stereo played, and music drifted almost lazily on the wind.

"He's not right to turn his back on the future," Luke said softly.

"No, he's not." There must be a compromise, but he and his grandfather had to really talk to find it. "I'm not saying you're completely wrong, or that he's completely right. I'm just saying that maybe the world has enough room for technology *and* teddy bears. Imagination is important, too, right?"

"Of course it is," he agreed with a half-smile. "But my toys don't destroy imagination."

"No, but your designers make such great games and tech toys, the kids don't have to use their *own* imaginations because your guys did it for them." She moved in closer and hooked both hands behind his neck. "Maybe there's a middle ground."

"If there is," he muttered, as his arms snaked around her waist, "I haven't found it yet."

Tipping her head to one side, she met his gaze and asked quietly, "Have you really looked?"

He stared into her eyes for what felt like forever. She couldn't read his thoughts, but the expression on his face clearly said he wasn't happy. Finally, he said, "No, I guess I haven't. I was so busy trying to prove I was right, I never really thought about meeting him halfway. Or even if there *is* a halfway."

She smiled at him and told herself not to celebrate. This didn't mean he'd go back to his family company. But it did mean he was willing to consider his options and maybe that was enough.

"You could talk to your grandfather…"

Nodding, he admitted, "I do miss that old hard-head."

She grinned. "I envy you your family, Luke. I never had that. When I was a child, I would have given anything for a family of my own. And, like you just said, he's getting old. Do you really want to let this keep you apart until it's too late to fix it?"

His features tightened, and she could see that

she'd given him more to think about. She was glad. Everything she'd said hadn't just been to serve this job. After Jamison hired her, Fiona had done research on kids and electronics, and some of the statistics had worried her.

She knew Luke was excited about this road he was on, but she thought that maybe he hadn't considered all the ramifications of pushing kids too hard into a digital world. If he was going to rethink some of his opinions, that was a good thing.

And maybe, she thought wistfully, one day, he'd look back on this time with her and smile. Maybe he wouldn't hate her once he'd found out she'd lied to him. Maybe…

"Why am I listening to you?" he asked, shaking his head.

"Because you're brilliant and insightful?"

"Yeah," he said, bending his head to kiss her. "That must be it."

Eight

The taste of her put everything else out of Luke's mind.

He liked talking to her. Even liked arguing with her, because she wasn't afraid to state her opinion and then defend it. She made him laugh. Made him think. Even about things he didn't want to consider.

But there was nothing like touching her. The rush of heat that overtook him every damn time kept him coming back to her. He didn't want or need a relationship. But for now, he needed Fiona.

He'd never meant for this—whatever it was between them—to continue beyond that long weekend in San Francisco. But the more time he spent with her, the more time he wanted with her. That thought should have worried Luke, and maybe it would. Later. But at the moment, all he could think was to feed the need devouring him.

Luke lost himself in Fiona just as he did every time he kissed her. Her scent, her taste, the hot, lush feel of her body pressed to his. He wanted it all. Wanted her more every time he had her.

Even with the icy ocean wind pummeling them from all sides, even with the lights of the house illuminating them for anyone to see, even with the fact that she'd just shot down some of his theories on technology for kids, he wanted her.

This kiss in the night wouldn't be enough. Tearing his mouth from hers, he looked down into chocolate-brown eyes that were swimming with passion and the kind of need that was nearly choking him.

"Come inside with me," he said, voice low and tight.

"Yes." She leaned into him more fully. "Oh, yes."

He gave her a quick grin, then grabbed her hand and tugged her along behind him. Across the patio, through the front door, and locked it after them. Up the stairs on the right to the landing and then down the hall to his bedroom.

Luke pulled Fiona into the room, then kicked the door shut behind them. She was laughing. Damn it, she was laughing and something inside him turned over. That wide smile, her bright brown eyes sparkling with humor and heat.

Of course he wanted her.

"In a hurry?" she finally asked, moving into his arms.

"Damn right I am," he assured her, pulling her in tight, using his hands, up and down her back to mold her body to his. He held her against his aching groin so she could feel exactly why he'd nearly run her legs off to get to this room with its massive bed.

"Me, too," she said, sliding her hands across his chest until he grabbed those hands and held them in a tight grip.

While they stood there, she looked around quickly. "I like your bedroom."

He knew what she was seeing. Pale gray walls, bookcases, flat-screen TV, forest green duvet covering his massive bed, and wide windows that overlooked the ocean. Because of those windows, Luke reached over and hit a switch on the wall. Instantly, heavy, dark green drapes slid soundlessly across the windows, throwing the room into darkness.

"Wow. A housekeeper. A cook. And you don't even have to close your own curtains," she whispered.

He grinned. "I did flip the switch."

"You're right. You're practically a frontiersman." She laughed again and everything in Luke fisted.

"Enough talking," he announced, and picked her up. She was tall, which he liked, and curvy, which he *really* liked, and she felt great in his arms.

He dropped her onto the bed and that amazing

laugh bubbled out of her again. He'd never been with a woman who laughed before, during and after sex. He liked it. It was somehow *more* because of that ease, that companionable laughter.

Luke switched on a bedside lamp because damn it, he wanted to see her. She lay stretched out across the bed like a beautifully wrapped present. Her black slacks and green long-sleeved shirt were like the wrappings, and he couldn't wait to undo it all.

As he watched, she undid the buttons on her shirt and then sat up to shrug it off, leaving behind only a pale pink lace bra that barely covered the breasts he wanted to indulge himself in.

"You're amazing," he muttered.

"I'm happy you think so," she whispered.

Luke tore his clothes off and tossed them onto a chair in the corner. Her eyes widened as she looked at him, and the expression on her face only fed the fires building inside him. Reaching down, he unhooked her slacks and slid them down and off her beautiful legs. The pale pink panties were next, and she lifted her hips to help him get them off. And then she was there, spread out before him like a feast.

Luke didn't waste a moment. He dragged her closer, then took her with his mouth. She gasped, lifted her hips again and cried out his name.

Sweetest sound he'd ever heard. Luke took his time, tasting, licking, nibbling at the core of her. Her heat swamped him, her shrieks and groans fed the need to give her more. To take more. He drove her to the ragged edge, while her fingers threaded through his hair and held his head to her. His hands cupped her butt and squeezed, his tongue swept over her innermost depths, and when he felt her nearly ready to shatter, he stopped.

"No, don't. Don't you dare leave me hanging like this." She lifted her head and fired a hard stare at him.

He grinned at her, then with a quick move, flipped her over onto her stomach. "Just getting started, Fiona."

She whipped her hair out of her face and looked back at him over her shoulder. "You're making me crazy."

"Well, it's about time. You've been doing that to me since we met."

Amazingly enough, she laughed again, and Luke told himself there was no one else like her. But who had time for revelations now?

"Up on your knees, Fiona…"

She stared at him for a long moment, then licked her lips in anticipation and did what he asked.

Still holding her gaze, he inched back off the bed and stood there a second or two before pulling her back toward him. When her butt was close enough, he smoothed his palms over it, squeezing, kneading, until she was moaning his name and rocking her hips in a futile search for the release he kept denying her.

Luke grabbed a condom from the bedside drawer, sheathed himself, then pushed himself deep inside her. Instantly, he groaned, and she gave a soft sigh of completion. It wasn't enough. It would never be enough. Being inside her heat, a part of her, yet separate, felt right. But the aching need to shatter pushed at him and Luke responded.

Again and again, he took her. He held her hips steady and moved his own, claiming her body, giving her his. He set a rhythm that she eagerly raced to meet. The only sounds in the room were their combined groans and the beautiful slap of flesh against flesh.

Luke gave himself over to the sensations pouring through him. He looked at her, listened to her and let her reactions multiply his own. When her gasping cries and shuddering body told him she was about to climax, he pushed her harder, faster until she called out his name on a high, thin scream and shattered in his hands.

A moment later, Luke let himself find the same shaking release, and he knew that nothing else would ever compare to what he shared with Fiona.

And as he swept her up into his arms, then lay down on the bed with her cuddled in close to his side, Luke realized that that admission should scare the hell out of him.

Later that night, Fiona stopped at Laura's because she had to talk to someone. Having that argument with Luke, fighting to make him see her side—his grandfather's side—had been nerve-racking. If she didn't push hard enough, nothing changed. If she pushed too hard, she'd lose him—even before she'd managed to complete her job and get him to go back to his family.

Then being with him, making love in that beautiful beach house, wrapped in his arms, feeling her own world shatter again and again. The whole night had filled her with an anxiety she didn't know how to deal with. She wanted this to be forever. And she knew it wouldn't—couldn't be. Because to stay with him, she'd have to confess to her lie. And if she did that, she'd lose him anyway. His was a world of black-and-white, right and wrong. And lying was wrong.

Mike answered the door. "Hey, Fiona."

He was wearing worn jeans and a black T-shirt. His hair was rumpled and whiskers stubbled his jaws.

"Hi, Mike. Sorry it's so late." Not really all that late. About eleven, but she still felt guilty for showing up out of the blue. Especially since Mike worked construction and would be out of the house at the crack of dawn.

"No problem." He pushed the screen door open and waved her inside. "Laura's in the kitchen baking cookies."

When Fiona looked at him in confusion, he shrugged.

"I don't ask why anymore." Smiling, he said, "Go on back. Have a cookie."

"Right. Thanks." She walked through the living room and found Laura, as promised, taking a tray of cookies out of the oven. Fiona wasn't even tempted to grab one, which only proved how torn up she was inside.

Laura looked up and blew a lock of hair out of her

eyes. "Hey, you're home early. Usually when you're with Luke it's a lot later—or even," she said with a grin, "the next morning."

"I've got an early job in Lakewood tomorrow."

Laura nodded. "Cookie?"

"No, thanks." She slid onto a barstool beneath the island counter.

"Uh-oh. If chocolate chip cookies can't tempt you, something is seriously wrong."

"Pretty much." Fiona braced both elbows on the granite counter and covered her face with her hands. Too many different emotions were stirring inside her at once. The memory of being with Luke made her blood burn, but the memory of talking to him, trying to make him change his mind about his family, his business, made her want to come clean. Her lie of omission was tearing at her. "It's a mess."

"Start talking." Laura set the hot tray onto the stove top to cool off, then went for a bottle of wine in the fridge. She poured two glasses, handed one to Fiona, took a sip of her own and waited.

"I don't even know where to start." She was in so deep now, she couldn't imagine a way out. Even if she told Luke the truth now, would it be enough to make up for lying to him for so long?

And wouldn't it put him and his grandfather at odds, too, if he found out the older man had hired someone to bring him back to the business?

Fiona stared at the sunlight-colored wine and finally drank some, if only to ease the tightness in her throat. "It's Luke."

"Yes." Laura leaned both elbows on the countertop. "I cleverly deduced that. What about him?"

Fingers absently twirling the stem of her wineglass, Fiona muttered, "I think I've about convinced him to make up with his grandfather."

"That's good news," Laura said, until Fiona's gaze met hers. Then she added, "Or not."

She gave her friend a strained smile. "No, it is. It really is. I mean, that is why his grandfather hired me. So that's good. But, Laura, there's a problem."

"You're in love with him."

Gaping at her best friend, Fiona could only nod. "I don't know how you know when I only just figured it out myself on the way home."

Laura patted her hand. "Oh, Fiona, it wasn't hard. You light up when you see him. You talk about him all the time. And you look at him like I look at Mike."

"Oh God." She scooped one hand through her still-windblown hair and took another drink of her wine. "This wasn't supposed to happen."

"Everybody says that." Laura took another sip of wine and shrugged.

"This is different, though." Shaking her head, she had another sip of wine and felt the cool slide through her system. "This started out as a job. I wasn't supposed to care about him, let alone *love* him. Plus, I've been lying to him, Laura. Right from the beginning."

She shrugged. "So tell him the truth."

"I can't do that."

"Why not? It's not exactly a wild idea."

Probably not to most rational people, but Fiona was feeling far from rational at the moment. "But if I tell him, I'll lose him. Not to mention that he'd be furious with his grandfather and how can I do that? Luke has hard lines between right and wrong, and a lie from me is going to fall on the 'wrong' side for sure."

"Hard lines get erased or moved all the time."

"Not by Luke."

Laura set her glass aside. "Sweetie, if you don't tell him, you've lost him anyway. You'll never really have him because you'll have that lie between you and it will make you crazy."

She was right, and Fiona really didn't want her to be right.

"Or worse, what if his family tells him what's been going on? What if he makes up with his grandfather and the old man brags about how he hired you to make it happen?"

Well, that was a horrifying thought. Fiona didn't believe Jamison would do that, because he wouldn't look good, either. But it could happen; her secret wasn't safe.

"Telling him the truth is really your only shot."

"And I really don't want it to be," Fiona admitted. God, she could still feel Luke's arms around her. Taste his mouth on hers. The thought of losing him now was almost more than she could take.

"Honey, I know that." Laura turned and grabbed

two still-warm cookies off the tray and handed one to Fiona. "But at least once it's done, you'll know where you really stand."

Fiona took a bite because she felt obligated, but as good a baker as Laura was, the cookie tasted like sawdust. Fiona didn't have to find out where she would stand when she told Luke the truth. She knew exactly where she would be standing.

On the outside looking in.

By the following afternoon, Luke was more torn than ever. He left work early because he just couldn't concentrate. Fiona stayed in his mind all the time now. Not just images of her, or the memories of incredible sex. It was her words haunting him, too. Everything she'd said the night before kept echoing in his brain, forcing him to sort through too many thoughts at once, struggling to make sense of everything and find the right path to take.

It wasn't just Fiona, either. Since meeting her, he'd become more aware, somehow. He'd noticed how people were attached to their phones. He saw little kids in restaurants, eyes on screens filled with laughing cartoon characters or brightly colored patterns. He realized that technology, while a boon to civilization—which he still believed—also had a downside.

It could keep families from staying connected.

Standing on his patio, staring out at the ocean, Luke had to wonder if his brilliant idea to hook small children on technology was the right path to take. He still believed technology was the wave of the future and that he wanted to be a part of it.

But everything Fiona had said to him the night before had sparked enough concern that he'd done more research of his own—all morning. And what he'd found had him second- and third-guessing himself. She'd been right about all of it. Kids were getting more and more isolated. Teen anxiety and depression rates were up, and toddlers were turning up with language delays after spending too much time with screens and not enough time talking with the grown-ups caring for them.

Scowling now, he took a sip of coffee and watched a lone surfer grab a wave and ride it to shore. "Another thing Fiona was right about," he muttered. "I'm going to miss being right on the ocean like this."

But wasn't that quandary a lot like his other problem at the moment? To live on the beach meant putting up with thousands of strangers staring in his windows or tossing trash onto his patio. Like being too involved with electronics cost a kid his own imagination. His own dreams.

He was moving to a cliffside house to protect his privacy. He was giving up what looked great for the right to make his life what he wanted it to be. Shouldn't he give his customers the same chance? By pushing tablets and screens on small children, wasn't he metaphorically tossing trash onto their patios?

"Damn it, Fiona." He gulped at his coffee and felt the burn as it scalded its way down his throat.

Do you really want to let this keep you apart until it's too late to fix it?

Her words had been circling his brain for hours.

Of course he didn't want Jamison to die with this stupid argument between them. Hell, he didn't want Jamison to die, period. And Luke was half convinced the old man was immortal. He was always so strong. So confident. So totally in control.

And Luke had turned out just like him. No wonder they clashed. Neither one of them was willing to give an inch. Back either one of them into a corner and they'd fight like mad to hold on to what they thought was right. Which meant that neither of them had ever learned how to bend.

On that thought, Luke pulled his phone from his back pocket and hit speed dial for his grandfather's office.

"Barrett."

"Cole?" Luke asked, recognizing his cousin's voice instantly. "What are you doing answering Pop's phone?"

"Pop's not here today," Cole said. "He took a personal day."

"Has there been an apocalypse nobody told me about?" Luke frowned at the phone. "Pop never takes a day off."

Cole sighed heavily. "He's eighty years old, Luke.

For God's sake, can't the man take a nap without your say-so?"

"He's *napping*?" Something was wrong. Jamison lived on about five hours sleep a night. Always had. And he had more energy than any ten men. Naps? Personal days? This was not Jamison Barrett.

"Did you expect him to live forever?" Cole countered. "He's an old man. You left and that changed everything for him. But I'm still here so I'm helping out."

That stung. Mostly because it was true. "Fine. Is he at home?"

"Yes, and don't call him."

"Excuse me?" Anger buzzed around like a hornet inside his mind.

"He needs the rest, Luke. He doesn't need you calling to argue with him again." Cole took a breath and said, "Look, I didn't want to say anything, but Pop's furious with you. Feels like you deserted him."

Regret and pain tangled together inside him, but Luke didn't argue with Cole. What would be the point? Besides, it wasn't his cousin he had to talk to. It was Pop.

"Just leave him be."

More emotions gathered inside him, nearly choking him. Since when did Cole call the shots not only for the company but for the family? "Yeah, thanks. Think I'll talk to him anyway."

"You would," Cole said. "Never think about the old man. Just do what Luke wants. That sounds right."

There was more bitterness than usual in his voice

and Luke wondered what else was going on. "What's your problem, Cole?"

"Same as always," his cousin said. "You." He hung up before Luke could say anything.

"Well, damn. Things have gone downhill fast." He'd talked to his grandfather just before the San Francisco trip and he'd been fine. Pissed off, but fine. A little more than a week later, to hear Cole tell it, Jamison was at death's door and Cole was the new sheriff in town.

Luke turned his face into the wind, hoping that the icy air would sweep away all the conflicting, troubling thoughts. Naturally, it didn't work. He had some things to do, but when he was finished, he'd be going to his grandparents' house to settle things.

Jamison had had enough. Damned if he'd sit back and wait for the proverbial ax to fall. He had always been a big believer that it was better to *know* something than to worry or guess about it.

And the last straw had been that contract that he'd supposedly signed. He knew damn well he hadn't. So what the hell was going on with him?

"I hate doctors' offices," he muttered. Impersonal, almost terrifying places that were cold, clinical, where the pale green walls seemed to have absorbed years of worry and then echoed it back into whoever happened to be in there. He shot a dirty look at the examination table and stayed right where he was in the most uncomfortable chair in the world. "I hate being here."

"Hey, me, too." Dr. Bill Tucker walked in, closed the door and then sat down on a chair opposite Jamison. "What say we blow this place?"

Jamison grinned in spite of the situation. Bill Tucker had been his doctor for twenty years. Somewhere in his sixties, Bill had gray hair, kind brown eyes and a permanent smile etched onto his face. Not one of those plastic *it'll be all right* smiles, but a real one. And today, Jamison needed to see it.

"What's going on, Jamie? Didn't expect to see you until your physical in a couple months."

"This couldn't wait." God, he hated this. Hated thinking he was losing his mind. Hated even more that someone might be trying to *convince* him he was going crazy.

Jamison had created what he'd always thought of as a family atmosphere at Barrett's. Had one of the people who'd worked for him for years turned on him? Why? It was the only thing that could explain what was happening to him, though he hated to consider it.

Bill gave him a rare frown. "Okay, tell me."

Jamison did, and as he told the story, he began to feel better. More in control. He wasn't being a passive observer to his own destruction anymore. He was finally doing something about it.

By the time he was finished, Bill wasn't smiling, but he didn't look worried, either.

"Jamie, that's a strange tale." He sat back and seemed to be mulling over his thoughts. "I don't think you've got anything to worry about, but we'll do some tests. Starting with the SLUMS cognitive test."

"Slums?"

Bill smiled again. "It's an acronym for the Saint Louis University Mental Status test. It's fast and will give us an idea of whether or not further testing will be necessary."

Worry erupted in his belly again, but this time Jamison pushed it aside. He was done agonizing without information. If there was something wrong, he'd fix it. Or find someone who could.

"Fine. When do we start?"

Bill nodded sharply. "I'll go get the test, and we can start right away."

Alone again, Jamison went over the whole strange story in his mind and tried to figure out exactly when things had started going badly. He couldn't pin it down to a specific day, but he knew damn well that he'd been fine a couple of months ago.

"And I'm fine now, too."

He needed to believe it, because anything else was just unacceptable.

Fiona had spent the morning tracking down a band that had once played at her client's high school dance, because the client wanted the same band to play at her wedding. In the last few years, that band had built an audience and, now, it spent a lot of time on the road, opening for bigger acts. Fiona's client knew the odds of making this happen were long, but she really wanted it because she and her fiancé had met at one of those school dances.

It should have taken forever, but Fiona had a friend in the business who gave her the number of the band's agent.

Once she explained the request to the woman, she put Fiona in touch with the band's lead singer. He was so flattered at the request, he not only agreed to do the wedding, but he wasn't going to charge them a thing. Especially after Fiona pointed out to him that a story like this was publicity gold.

The bride was ecstatic at the news, but once that call had been made, Fiona was left with her own troubling thoughts again. She had to tell Luke the truth. But before she did that, it was only fair that she let Jamison Barrett know what she was planning. She hoped he would understand, though she knew he might not, since Luke would be furious not only with her, but with his grandfather.

But there was no other choice. If she wanted a chance at long-term with Luke, and she did, then she had to remove the lie standing between them like a solid wall.

She didn't have to meet her next client for an hour, so there was no time like now to get the chat with Jamison over and done.

Fiona dialed, took a deep breath and let it out when a familiar voice said simply, "Fiona."

"Yes." As usual, she paced aimlessly in her apartment and for the first time, wished for more space.

Wished she were at Luke's house so she could simply walk out onto the sand and feel the wind in her face.

"Now isn't the best time." His voice was short. Tense. "But I'll be calling you tomorrow to talk about a new job."

"What?" She hadn't been expecting that at all. He sounded better than he had the last time she spoke with him, and she was glad of it. But it was the current job she had to talk to him about. "Mr. Barrett…"

"Sorry, Fiona, no time." He hung up and Fiona was left hanging again.

"Now what?" she muttered darkly.

He had "no time" to hear about the job he'd hired her for? That didn't make sense. And he wanted to hire her for something else? What was going on with Luke's grandfather? And oh boy, did she wish she could talk to Luke about all of this. But she couldn't. Because of the lies.

Which brought her back to: she had to tell Luke everything and try to explain. Just the thought of that turned her stomach and made her regret ever getting into this in the first place. Although if she hadn't accepted the job from Jamison Barrett, she never would have met Luke at all.

God, she had a headache.

If she didn't tell Luke soon, he might find out on his own. And that would be worse. But if she did tell him without first telling his grandfather, that wouldn't be fair to the older man.

She was still caught. Trapped. In her own lie.

Nine

"Mr. Barrett. I didn't expect you here today."

Luke glanced at the other man. One of his top marketing guys, David Fontenot, was tall, blond and tanned. As the head of market research for Luke's new company, Dave ran the focus groups brought in to try out their new products. He knew how to read the kids' reactions to the tech they were introduced to and knew exactly how to push those products in the best markets.

"I wanted to come and watch the focus group for myself this time." He'd been getting reports, of course, from Dave himself, the observers, designers, graphic artists. But given the conversation he and Fiona had had the night before, Luke had decided it was time to get some firsthand information.

"Sure." Dave waved one hand down the hall and started walking. "I'll show you where you can sit and watch. We've got a group of six kids for today."

"How old?"

Dave winced, then laughed. "This is the toddler bunch. I'll tell you right off that getting the younger kids to settle down and pay attention is a little like trying to herd cats."

Luke lifted one eyebrow. "Aren't the tablets supposed to do that? Engage young minds, get them to learn?"

"Of course. Sure." Dave spoke quickly, explaining. "But first, we have to get them to notice the tablets. And the truth is, I think the toddlers scare Andy—he's our guy in the room. They're a little overwhelming—"

"So get someone else in there."

He laughed and shook his head. "Yeah, that's the thing. Mr. Barrett, we can't get anyone else to volunteer to be in the middle of toddlers. The older kids? No problem. Plenty of volunteers." He shrugged. "Andy will get the job done, though. I promised him I'd buy his coffee for a week."

"Good bribe," Luke said, approving.

"Not for me, since I'll be paying, and he drinks a lot of coffee." Dave opened a door at the end of the hallway and showed Luke into a tiny room with four empty chairs. "You can stay here. This is one of three observation rooms."

"Thanks." Luke didn't usually come down here

to the satellite office in Irvine. Marketing, research and design were located here but he was able to stay on top of everything through email and phone calls.

He checked his watch. "When does it start and how long will it last?"

Dave took his phone out to check the time. "The kids will be going inside any minute and with the toddlers, we don't go longer than a half hour." He shrugged and grinned. "By then they want a drink or a nap or a banana."

For participating in the focus groups, the kids would get a toy and their parents received gift cards for any restaurant they chose. And hopefully, Luke and his team would get the information they needed to perfect their toys and tablets.

Dave nodded. "There they are now."

Luke watched six tiny kids race into the room. The area was filled with beanbag chairs, small tables littered with paper and crayons, and of course, his company's toys and tablets. For toddlers, the tablets were practically unbreakable and came in cases that were in bright primary colors.

Andy, the volunteer who apparently wished he were anywhere else, did his best to steer the kids toward the tablets, and four of the six complied. They turned on the tablets, and bright patterns and storyboards sailed across the screens. Those four toddlers immediately sat down to study the program playing, and Luke watched as they settled down and focused on the screen pattern.

The other two kids, though, chased each other

around the small play area while Andy tried unsuccessfully to corral them.

Luke smiled to himself at the sound of the giggles streaming through the speakers. Two out of six were playing, coloring, jumping onto the beanbag chairs. And he suddenly remembered Laura's son, Travis, running across the yard chasing a ball while the neighbor kids sat on a porch lost in their screens.

He could almost hear Fiona's voice in his ear, talking about kids playing, using their imaginations. He could see her eyes, staring up into his, and he heard her telling him to take a chance at compromise with his grandfather.

She was right, he thought, and felt a twinge in his heart he hadn't expected.

And as he continued to study the kids, he realized there was a stark difference between those four children, mesmerized by the flashing colors and dancing bears—and the two free spirits now trying to color Andy's khaki slacks.

He stayed through the whole half hour and when he left, he found Dave. "Tell Andy the company's buying his coffee for a month. He earned it."

Laughing, Dave went back to work, and Luke stepped into the afternoon sunlight. His mind was racing, bouncing from one thought to the next as he began to rethink his own opinions on kids and tech.

Maybe it was time to go see Pop.

Jamison felt better than he had in weeks.

Except for the fury.

"Loretta," he snapped, "*someone* at the company's been trying to gaslight me and doing a damn fine job of it."

It infuriated him that he'd bought into the whole thing. He should have had more confidence in his own damn mind. But whoever was behind this had counted on him reacting just as he had. As you got older, there was no greater fear than losing your marbles. Forget *anything* and the word *Alzheimer's* sailed into your brain along with the terror that word invoked.

"There has to be another explanation," his wife said from her chair in his study.

"Like what?" He tossed both hands up and shook his head fiercely. "Some stupid practical joke that nobody laughed at? What other possible explanation is there except that someone wanted me to think I was losing my mind?"

Since taking that SLUMS test at the doctor's office, Jamison knew his mind was as sharp as ever. Bill hadn't even bothered with other tests once he'd seen the results. The doctor had sent him home with a clean bill of health, thank God. But now he was forced to get to the bottom of a mystery.

Idly, he jingled the change in his pants pockets until the sound began to rattle him. He stopped, stared into space and tried to get a grip on the anger surging through him. Even Loretta's calming nature couldn't quell it. Not this time.

"Jamie," she asked, "who would do it?"

"I don't know," he admitted, shooting a glance at

his wife. The not knowing was gnawing a hole in his gut. At this rate, he'd have his mind but would soon gain an ulcer.

Outside, the winter sky was as dark as Jamison's thoughts. He'd been betrayed. By someone he trusted. And that was a hard thing to accept.

"By God, most of our employees have been with us more than twenty years," he murmured. "Why suddenly would any one of them turn on me like this?"

Loretta folded her arms across her chest and hugged herself tightly. Shaking her head, she said, "It can't be someone we know."

"It has to be," Jamison countered. He knew what she was feeling, because he was feeling the same thing. Neither of them wanted to believe that someone they'd known and trusted for years would do something like this. But it was the only answer. "Who else would know how to forge my signature? Or do any of the other things that were done to me? It's someone close to me."

He paused. "Donna?"

"Oh, please." Insulted for the woman who had been their friend for decades, Loretta said hotly, "You might as well suggest it's Cole as Donna. I'll never believe she is capable of this."

"But we can say that about everyone at the company." He scrubbed one hand across the back of his neck. "Tim in marketing? Sharon in accounting? Phillip in purchasing? I'll tell you the truth, Loretta. This is a damn nightmare."

Loretta stood up, walked to her husband and wrapped her arms around him for a quick hug. "We'll find out what's going on."

He patted her back. "It won't change anything, but damn right we will. Someone in my own damn company was trying to sabotage me. Get me thinking I was senile or something. I need to know who." He thought about it for a minute. "I can't come right out and ask anybody, because they'd all deny it. So, we'll have to be sneaky about it."

"I hate this," Loretta murmured, stepping back from him to stare into his eyes.

"So do I," Jamison admitted. "But it has to be done, and there is one person who might be able to get to the bottom of this. Fiona Jordan."

"Who's that?" Loretta asked.

"How do you know Fiona?" Luke demanded.

Luke stared at his grandfather and, to his credit, the old man didn't look away. But he knew his grandfather well enough to see the shock and shame glittering in his eyes. As if it were a living, breathing entity in the room, Luke sensed *guilt* hovering right behind his grandfather as if trying to go unnoticed.

"Luke, sweetheart, it's so good to see you!" Loretta smiled and gave him a hug.

"Hello, Gran." He held on to her for a moment, then let her go and fired another hard look at the man who'd raised him.

Jamison Barrett was a law unto himself. He did

what he thought was right and didn't care what anyone had to say about it. But Luke knew him too well to be thrown by the bravado in the old man's eyes. There was something here, and he wasn't leaving until he found out what it was.

"Good to see you, boy."

"Uh-huh. How do you know Fiona Jordan, Pop?" Luke kept his gaze fixed on the older man's. He saw the flash of unease in Jamison's eyes and knew that whatever was coming, he wasn't going to like it. In his own head, Luke was putting things together quickly and he didn't like what he was finding.

Meeting a gorgeous woman at a tech conference in San Francisco when she had no real reason to be at that hotel? She'd said she was there on business, but what were the odds of someone in Northern California hiring a woman from Long Beach to do anything?

He smelled a setup.

Betrayal snarled inside him. Were Fiona and Pop conspiring together against him? God, he was an idiot. Fiona had been lying to him all this time. What the hell else had she lied about?

"Well," Jamison said, and jingled the change in his pocket.

Luke frowned. The jingling was a nervous habit when Jamison was trying to think or when he was uneasy.

"Fiona did some business for Donna not too long ago. Found her sister's long-lost daughter."

"It's true," Loretta said, laying one hand on her heart. "It was lovely to see Donna's sister Linda so happy after all those years."

Fiona had told him about that job. She hadn't mentioned that she'd done it for his grandfather's secretary's sister. All the time they'd talked about Jamison and she'd never once mentioned that she had a connection through Donna?

Coincidence? Luke didn't think so.

"Right. So, you didn't hire her?" Luke asked.

The change jingling got louder. Jamison rocked on his heels and did everything he could to avoid eye contact.

"You did, didn't you?" Luke pushed one hand through his hair in frustration. "You hired her. You sent her to San Francisco to ambush me."

His grandfather rubbed his jaw.

"My God, Pop. What the hell won't you do to get your way?"

"Jamie?" Loretta asked warily, "Is he right? Did you do something you should be ashamed of?"

Jamison looked from one to the other of them and even through the anger spiking inside him, Luke could see the old man trying to find a way out of this.

Luke wasn't going to let him. "Damn it, Pop, just admit that you did it. You hired Fiona to seduce me into coming back to the company."

"What?" He looked genuinely shocked at the accusation. "I did not. I hired her to get you to come back, yes. If you were seduced, that's on you."

"Jamie, how could you?" Loretta gave her husband a smack on the arm.

"What else could I do?" he argued. Pointing at Luke, he continued, "The boy wouldn't listen to me. I was afraid he'd never come back, and I needed him."

"You're unbelievable." Luke could hardly talk. He was furious. He'd been used by his family, lied to by his lover. His stomach was in knots, and his heart was hammering in his chest.

What the hell was going on here?

"You left me no choice."

"The choice was to butt the hell out."

Jamison waved that away. "That wasn't going to happen."

"Of course not." Through the rage, the sense of betrayal, Luke could admit that he should have seen this coming. His grandfather would always do whatever he had to do to get his way. He'd been doing it his whole life. Hell, he'd taught Cole and Luke both to go after what they wanted and never take no for an answer.

It had never occurred to Luke, though, that meeting Fiona was anything other than a happy accident. Had she *planned* to fall into his lap? Was the sex all about the job? Did she sleep with all of her clients or targets?

Damn it, he'd fallen for her whole act. That laugh of hers. Her eyes. Her kiss. He'd *listened* to her. Respected her opinion, and it was all a lie. Hell, for all he knew, she loved the idea of tech for kids, and everything she'd said to him about it had been scripted by his grandfather. He'd actually been tempted to build something with Fiona. In spite of not wanting a relationship, he'd been leaning toward breaking that personal rule. And this is what it got him.

"This is low, Pop," he ground out, gaze pinning the older man. "Even for you."

Jamison didn't like that and scowled to prove it. "If you'd just listened to me."

"Jamie, you never should have done this," Loretta snapped, glaring at the man she loved. "Apologize this instant."

"Damned if I will. I did what needed doing." Jamison shot a hard look at his grandson. "I'm eighty years old, boy. You think I'm going to live forever? If you don't come back, the family company will go under."

"Oh no," Luke told him. "You don't get to lay this on me. Cole is more than ready to take it over."

"We both know Cole couldn't do the job. It's *you* I needed, and you damn well knew it when you walked out." Jamison was just as mad as Luke. and the two of them stood there glaring at each other.

"I left to prove something to myself. And to you," Luke snapped. "I didn't do it to ruin your plans—"

"Well you did anyway."

"Jamie!"

"They were *your* plans," Luke argued. "Not mine."

"And that's what this is about? A tantrum? You don't like taking orders, so you just run off?"

"Jamie, stop," Loretta ordered.

"I didn't run. I left. You know the irony is," Luke countered, gritting his teeth and narrowing his gaze on the man he admired more than anyone else in his life, "I was actually coming here today to say maybe you were right. Maybe we should work together at the family company. Find a compromise."

Jamison's eyes lit up.

"*Then* I find out you set me up."

"Oh hell," Jamison argued, "that doesn't change what you've come to believe, does it? True is true no matter how you come to it."

Loretta sighed. "Jamie, I'm so disappointed in you. You can't run our boys' lives no matter how much you want to. What were you thinking?"

He turned on his beloved wife then. "I was thinking that I heard my wife crying in the shower when she thought I couldn't hear her over the water running."

Luke snorted. "Gran doesn't cry." Then he looked at her and saw the truth on her face. "You *cried*?"

Frowning at Jamison, she stabbed her index finger at him. "You shouldn't have said anything. That was private. And stop listening at the bathroom door, it's rude."

He went to her, rubbed his hands up and down her arms and said, "I was worried about you, is all. And I knew I had to get him—" he jerked a thumb at Luke "—back for both our sakes."

Luke shoved his hands through his hair. He was

angry and regretful and furious and guilty and realizing that maybe he'd had a huge hand in all of this happening. He hated thinking that Gran had been brought to tears over what he'd done. He owed her better than that. And Pop had only done what he'd always done. Rush in to handle a situation the best way he knew how.

That might excuse his grandfather, but it sure as hell didn't excuse Fiona. She'd lied to him. He felt like a damn fool. Every minute of time he had spent with her had been bought and paid for by his grandfather.

She had come to mean a lot to him. Now he had to face the fact that all of that was a lie as well. Where that left him, he didn't know.

Shaking his head, Luke promised himself to take this up with her later. He would have the truth. Finally. From everyone. For now, there was his grandfather to deal with.

Taking a deep breath, Luke shoved his hands into his pants pockets and stared at the old man watching him warily. "Leaving all the rest of it alone, what are you hiring Fiona for now?"

Jamison eyed him. "Does this mean you're back?"

"God, you're a hardhead." Luke threw both hands in the air. "Even when I find out what you've been doing all you're interested in is, *am I coming back?*"

"Well, why wouldn't I want to know? That's what it's all been for. So, are you?"

Blowing out a breath, Luke said only, "It means

I'm here now, and I haven't left even though I'm so mad at you I can't see straight."

Clearly insulted, Jamison muttered, "Well, that seems an exaggeration."

"Jamie!" Gran slapped one hand to her own forehead in clear exasperation and, suddenly, Luke felt all kinds of respect for the woman who could put up with Jamison Barrett for nearly sixty years.

Scowling, Jamison admitted, "Fine. We'll leave it for now. As to your question, I need Fiona to find out who's been trying to drive me out of my mind." He was jingling again.

"What are you talking about, Pop?"

Jamison started talking then, words rushing together, and with every word his grandfather said, Luke's anger became cold as ice. Who the hell would torture an old man like that? Make him doubt himself?

Too many lies, he told himself. Too many people who couldn't be trusted. He'd find who had been trying to destroy Pop. He'd even use Fiona to get it done.

But first, he was going to have a talk with the woman who'd been lying to him from the moment they met.

Fiona finished typing up three résumés for new clients, then baked a pan of brownies for a neighbor's birthday party and ended the day by returning a lost dog to its very happy owner. Of course, she still had to design baby announcements and one save-the-date card for two other clients, but those jobs would be fun.

She loved the creativity of what she did and, mostly, she loved being busy. Because at the moment, keeping her mind occupied meant she didn't have time to worry about what would happen when she talked to Luke.

Fiona had tried to make plans for exactly *how* to tell him the truth. No matter what she came up with though, it didn't sound right. Over a drink? During dinner? After sex? She wouldn't want to tell him *before* sex, or it might not happen again.

The sad truth was, she didn't want to tell Luke at all. In her fantasies, her lies were buried, Luke loved her, and they lived happily ever after. But fantasy rarely had anything at all to do with reality. So, she was left with her only choice.

Confessing all and watching him walk away.

When she pulled into the driveway that afternoon, it seemed almost cosmic, then, to find Luke sitting on her front porch, waiting for her. Her stomach jumped and her heart gave a hard leap in her chest.

He wore one of his amazing suits, with the top collar button of his shirt undone and his dark green tie hanging loose. He had one arm resting on his upraised knee and as she approached, he narrowed his gaze on her until she felt as if she were under a microscope.

"Luke? I wasn't expecting to see you tonight."

"Yeah. Thought I should come by and tell you that I talked to my grandfather today."

Her heartbeat skittered into a frantic beat. She swallowed hard and forced a smile. "That's wonderful. Did you work everything out?"

"Not nearly." He stood up and loomed over her, forcing Fiona to tip her head back to meet his gaze. "But you'll be happy to know that Pop is planning on hiring you again since you did such a great job with *me*."

Did the earth open up under her feet? Is that why she felt that sinking sensation? Staring into his eyes, she wanted to look away, but didn't. She saw the accusation, the anger, there and knew this talk was going to be every bit as bad as she'd feared it would.

"Oh God. Luke… I wanted to tell you—"

"But you just couldn't find the time?" Sarcasm and a hard expression.

Fiona shook her head, dug in her purse for her keys and said, "Just let me open the door. Come inside. I'll explain everything."

She squeezed past him and he didn't budge an inch.

"Can't wait to hear it."

She felt him behind her. Judgment and anger were rolling off him in thick waves, and she couldn't even blame him. Her hands shook so badly she couldn't get the stupid key into the stupid lock. But maybe part of that was psychological. She knew that the minute they were inside, the argument would start, and the end of her relationship with him would arrive.

"Let me do it." Luke reached around her for the

key. She gave it to him; he slid it home and opened the door. He was right behind her as she stepped into her house.

Fiona dropped her purse onto the closest chair, braced herself and turned to face him. "I know you're angry…"

"Oh," he assured her, "angry doesn't even come close to describing what I am right now."

One look into his eyes told her that. The cool blue was glinting with too many emotions to sort out. But his fury was obvious in the way he moved and stood.

"You have every right to be mad."

"Thanks so much."

She winced at the ice in his voice. "I was going to tell you myself tomorrow, Luke."

"Easy to say now."

"I know, but it's true." He wouldn't believe her, she knew. But then, why should he? "I hated lying to you."

"But you did it anyway. Impressive."

Fiona ignored that. "Yes, your grandfather hired me. I couldn't tell you that. Jamison was my client and I owed him confidentiality."

"And what did you owe me?"

"Luke, at first, it was just a job, but the moment I met you—"

"Let me guess," he said sarcastically. "Everything changed for you."

Helplessly, she threw her hands up. "Well, yeah."

"Don't, Fiona." He stopped her before she could

say more. "Just, don't. My grandfather paid you to talk me into going back to the family business. Everything else was just part of the dance."

His voice was cold and hard, and she couldn't even blame him. But oh, standing here with him, so close, but so far away from each other, was even worse than she'd imagined it would be.

"Not everything."

"Right. So, do you sleep with all your targets, or was I just lucky?"

She sucked in a gulp of air at the insult. He was hurting. He was pissed. He felt betrayed. Of course he was going to strike back. "I'm going to let that go because I know you're furious."

"Tell me, just how much did you charge the old man for having sex with me?"

Her head jerked back as if she'd been slapped. "He didn't pay me to care about you. Didn't pay me to sleep with you."

"Good, because we didn't do much sleeping, did we?"

Okay, she was willing to give a lot here because she was the one who'd screwed this all up. As soon as she'd realized she was coming to care for him, she should have told him everything. Should have been honest with him no matter what it had cost. But there was a limit to how much offense she was willing to put up with. Her own anger started as a flicker of heat in the pit of her stomach and quickly spread until she was swamped with it.

"You know what?" she snapped, taking a step toward him. "Insulting me isn't the answer here. Yes. I lied. Yes, I'm a horrible human being. But I didn't have sex with you for money."

"And I should believe you because you're so honest." Sarcasm dripped from his tone and if anything, his eyes became even icier.

"Do or don't," she said hotly. "That's up to you. But I'm not going to keep taking this from you, Luke. Are you so perfect that you've never done anything you regret? Are your hard lines of right and wrong so deeply drawn that you can't see that other people make difficult choices and don't always make the right ones?"

"Are you seriously trying to turn this around on me?" he countered.

"I didn't say that. I'm willing to take the blame for all of this—even though *you're* the one who put your grandfather into a situation where he felt the only way to solve it was to hire a stranger to talk to his own grandson!"

She enjoyed seeing a quick flash of guilt in his eyes, but it was gone an instant later.

Fiona felt bad about this whole situation. She had all along, but she wasn't going to stand there and not defend herself.

"I didn't decide to sleep with you easily. I've never done anything like that before. Heck, I've never slept with anyone as quickly as I did with you." She'd known all along that this was coming. She'd taken something for herself, for her own needs and desires and now, the bill was due. She had to accept the consequences, no matter how difficult. "And I wanted to pretend, I guess, that there was more between us than there was. I only had sex with you because I cared about you."

"Right."

"Do you think I could fake that? What we felt when we were together?" That hurt. Looking into his eyes and seeing only anger flashing there might have made it a little easier. But she saw pain there, too, and that told her he was having as hard a time with this as she was.

"How the hell do I know? You're a damn good liar."

"Now who's lying, Luke?" She met his gaze and stared him down. "I was there. I felt your response to me, and I know you were feeling everything I did."

"You don't know anything about me, Fiona," he said, bending lower so their faces were just a breath apart. "If you did, you wouldn't have lied to me."

"Yes. I lied. But not about everything."

"I don't believe you."

"Was it so wrong for me to be with you? To let myself feel? Think what you want to, you will anyway." She moved in closer to him, tipped her head back and met that icy blue stare unflinchingly. "But I took that job from your grandfather because it was for *family*." Even saying that word had tears burning at the backs of her eyes. "I never had what you turned your back on. I had exactly one person in my life who loved me. One. That's more than I ever thought I'd have.

"But you had a whole family who loved you. You had everything I used to dream about having and still you walked away from it all. You crushed your grandfather."

He snorted, but his expression said he worried she was right. "That old man is indestructible."

Sadly, she shook her head. "No one is, Luke. Jamison depends on you. Loves you. He's proud of you."

"This isn't about Pop," he pointed out.

"Part of it is," she countered. "He didn't want you to know that he'd hired me because he knew you would never listen if you did. So, this is mostly about you, Luke. You walked out on the people who loved you most. Well, your grandparents want you to come home. And I think you should."

"I think what I do is none of your business."

"Yes, you've made that clear enough." His words were like another slap, only this time to her heart. Fiona loved a man who would always see her as a liar. He would never understand what had driven her to be with him, even knowing that it was impossible for it to last. So, it was over. And emptiness rose up inside her like an incoming tide.

But he was still standing there, staring at her, and she couldn't help wondering why he hadn't left.

Why hadn't he stormed out, taking all of his righteous anger with him?

"Is there more?" she asked. "Have any other insults you'd like to toss around?"

"Quite a few, actually," he said tightly. "But I'll pass. Instead, I have another job for you from my grandfather."

"No, thank you. Go away." She wanted nothing more to do with the Barrett family.

"I think you owe me one," he said and that had her snapping him a look.

"How do I owe you anything?"

"Lies have a price, Fiona, and you told a boatload."

She took a step back from him because she couldn't stand being so close and not being able to touch him. Even now, her heart yearned for him and everything in her ached to wrap her arms around him and hold on. So, a little space between them was a very good thing.

"Fine. What does he want?"

"Someone at the company has been trying to convince Jamison he's crazy." Luke scowled at the thought. "Hiding things from him, canceling orders, ordering other things. They had him convinced he was sliding into dementia. He wants you to look into it. Do what you do. Talk to people. Find out who's behind it."

That was terrible, and now she at least knew why

Jamison had sounded so unsure of himself that time on the phone. Who would do something so vicious and heartless?

"I'll do it," she said. "Only because I like your grandfather."

"Fine. Let me know when you have something."

He couldn't have been more distant. His beautiful eyes were shuttered. His voice was clipped and raw. And still, she loved him. Knew she'd never love anyone else like this. Everything in Fiona ached to say the words. Just once, she wanted to say them and mean them and it didn't matter to her if he dismissed them, because he'd already dismissed *her*.

He opened the door, and Fiona knew she had to tell him because who knew if she'd ever have the chance to say those words again and really mean them. Her heart hurt because her best chance at a happily ever after was about to walk out her door. How could she not tell him how she felt?

"Luke."

He looked at her.

She took a breath and let it out again. "I only had sex with you because I fell in love with you."

His eyes flashed, and his mouth worked as if he were biting back words that were trying to tumble out.

"I just wanted to tell you that," Fiona said. "Because I've never said those words before, and I don't know if I'll ever have the chance again."

Still he didn't speak, but his gaze was fixed on her.

It didn't matter if he responded or not. She hadn't said those magical words for his sake, but for her own.

"But when this job is done," she said quietly, "I never want to see you again."

Ten

Luke hadn't seen Fiona in a week, and he missed her, damn it.

He shouldn't. She'd become the very distraction he had been trying to avoid. She'd lied to him from the beginning. Every conversation. Every laugh. Every kiss. Every... It was all built on lies.

And still, he wanted her. Thought about her. Missed her.

"Where's your mind, boy?" Jamison's voice cut into his thoughts, and Luke could have kissed his grandfather for the distraction.

"Right here," he said, looking at Pop from across the dining room table.

His grandparents' house hadn't changed in years.

And somehow that was comforting since everything else around him seemed to be a swirling vortex of chaos. For the last week, Luke and Jamison had worked here, at the house, coming up with a compromise. Luke believed that this time, they'd be able to find a way to walk a line between the past and the future, while encouraging kids to get outside and have adventures again.

It would have been easier to do all this at the office, but until they found out who was behind the mental attacks on Jamison, they weren't announcing Luke's return. Not even to Cole, because he'd never been very good at keeping a secret.

"Are you sure you want to keep your group of people working on the tech division?" Jamison shook his head and checked one of the papers strewn across the table. "Might be easier to fold them into the division we've already got."

"No," Luke said. He was willing to go back to Barrett. Thought it was a good idea, actually. But though the tech part of the business would be taking a back seat to more standardized toys, he wanted his hand-picked crew working on the technological side of things. Whatever tech toys they *did* produce would be top of the line.

"My people have some great ideas, and I'd like them to keep working on those right where they're at for now. We'll call it a research division of the company. Maybe later, we can revisit."

Jamison looked at him for a long moment, then

nodded, satisfied. "All right, then. We can talk about next year's lineup."

"That's fine, Pop." Better to focus. To think about work—that way thoughts of Fiona couldn't slip in to torture him.

"Have you heard from Fiona?"

He muffled a groan because it seemed he couldn't avoid thinking or talking about Fiona. "No. You?"

"Nothing," Jamison muttered, and tossed his pen down in disgust. "I was hoping she'd have something by now. I need to know who was doing that to me, Luke. Need to get rid of them so I can move forward knowing that everyone working for me is really working *for* me."

"I get it." Luke wanted to know, too. And then he planned on having a long chat with whoever had tried to submarine his grandfather.

"Well, then, call her, boy. Find out what she knows."

Luke went still. "She'll call when she has something."

"Is there a reason you're suddenly not interested in talking to the woman?"

Luke just stared at him for a long moment. "Yeah. She lied to me."

"They weren't her lies, they were mine."

Snorting, Luke shook his head. "Not all of them."

"The problem here is, you care for her."

"Nope, that's not it." Luke picked up the graphic sample of their fall ads. "What do you think about this? I'm thinking my graphic designer could find a way to make this stand out more."

"I'm thinking you're avoiding the subject."

"Good call," Luke told him. "So drop it."

"I would, but I like the girl."

Leaning back in his chair, Luke glared at him. "This time I'm just going to say it. Butt out, Pop."

"Well now," Jamison said with a wink, "we both know that's not going to happen."

Reaching for the coffee carafe, Luke poured himself another cup of the hot black brew and tried to ignore the older man across from him.

"When I met your grandmother, I knew right away that she was the one." He smiled to himself as if looking back through the years. "You know how?"

"No." But he guessed he was about to find out.

"Because she made me laugh," Jamison said. "She made me think. She made me a better man just by being around me."

Luke frowned at his coffee. He didn't want to hear this because it struck too close to home. Wasn't that exactly what Fiona had done for him? Hadn't she, just by being herself, made him reconsider everything he'd thought he'd believed?

Didn't her laughter make him smile? Her touch make him hunger? Her sighs feed something in his soul that had been empty before her?

He remembered the look on her face when he'd confronted her. Remembered the shock and the pain in her eyes when he'd suggested she'd had sex with him because it was her *job*.

Okay, yes, he'd been a colossal jerk, and she'd called him on it. But in his defense... Screw it, there was no defense.

Jamison was watching him, and the old man was way too cagey for Luke's liking. Whatever had been between him and Fiona was over. Whether it was her lies or his accusations, it was over and done now.

"Let it go, Pop. *Please*."

"Fine," he said, nodding. "For now."

At this point, Luke was willing to accept that.

Two days later, Fiona knocked on the front door of Luke's home. The roar of the sea seemed to match her thundering heartbeat, and the icy wind was the same temperature as her cold hands. Her stomach was a twisting, swirling mess and it felt like every cell in her body was on high alert. She felt brittle. As if she might shatter into pieces at any moment.

She'd completed her job, and though they might not like the answers she was offering them, once this task was done, the Barrett family would be out of her life for good. And that thought chilled her far more than the wind could.

The door swung open and there he was, just inches from her. Fiona took a deep breath to steady herself, but it didn't do any good. How could it, when all she had to do was look at Luke Barrett and her knees got wobbly and her heart began racing?

He wore a tight black T-shirt and worn jeans that rode low on his hips. He was barefoot and his hair was rumpled, making her wish she had the right to run her fingers through it. But those days were gone for good.

Still, she was glad she'd taken the time to dress for this meeting. She wore a dark green shirt with cap sleeves and a scoop neckline and the kicky black skirt she'd been wearing when she first dropped onto his lap. She knew the choice had been a good one when she saw his eyes flare dangerously.

"Fiona."

His voice sent a whisper of sensation drifting along her spine.

"Hello, Luke. I finished looking into your grandfather's problem."

One eyebrow lifted. "And?"

"And," she repeated, "I want to talk to you about it."

His gaze felt like a touch. It was intimate and distant all at once.

He opened the door wider, and she walked inside, being careful not to brush against him. How strange this was, she thought. They'd been as close as any two people could be and, now, they were less than strangers.

She knew her way around, so she walked directly into the living room. There were moving boxes everywhere, and her heart felt a sharp stab of regret. He was getting ready to leave this house and though she knew he was moving, she had no idea where. So, she'd never be able to find him again. That thought was a lonely one, but at the same time, she supposed it was for the best. Now she couldn't be tempted to drive past his house like some sad stalker, hoping to catch a glimpse of him.

Turning to face him, she handed him a manila envelope and when he opened it, she started talking. "I have a friend who's a computer genius."

"Of course you do."

She ignored that. "With Jamison's permission, he hacked into the system at Barrett's and tracked everything he could. There were what he called 'footprints' left behind and when he followed them, he found the person responsible for hurting your grandfather."

Luke looked at the papers, then lifted his gaze and shook his head. "This can't be right."

"It is," she assured him. "We checked everything twice, to make sure. I'm sorry, Luke."

His gaze hardened instantly, and she was sad to see it.

"I don't want another apology."

"I'm sorry about *this*." Fiona straightened up, squaring her shoulders, lifting her chin. "As for the other thing, I've already apologized once, and I won't do it again."

"Is that right?"

"Yes, Luke." She moved in close enough that she could see every shift of emotion in his eyes. "Normal people screw up and when they do, they apologize, are forgiven and the world goes on."

"So now this is my fault." He snorted and shoved the paperwork back into the envelope.

"I didn't say that." Sighing, she shook her hair back behind her shoulders. He wouldn't bend. Wouldn't understand that what she'd done had been hard for her. That it had torn at her. That it was more complicated than black-and-white. It wasn't that he *couldn't* forgive her. He chose not to. "I don't think you'll ever find anyone perfect enough to live in your idealized world, and that's a shame."

He stiffened, and his features went cold and hard. "I didn't ask for your sympathy, either."

"Too bad. You've got it anyway." She paused to steady herself so she could say and believe the hard truth. "It's over, Luke. No matter who's at fault, it's over. I know that and so do you. That's really the only thing that counts now."

She took one long last look into those summer-blue eyes of his, then left while she still could.

"I'm sorry about this, Pop." An hour later, Luke watched his grandfather read over the paperwork Fiona had given him, and he could have sworn he saw the old man age right before his eyes.

And Luke could have punched his cousin in the face for that alone.

"Can't believe Cole would do all of this," Jamison

muttered. "I never would have guessed it was him. Which is why, I suppose, he was able to do it."

"There must be a reason," Loretta mused aloud, as if trying to reassure herself.

There was a gas fire dancing in the hearth against the February cold, but it didn't do a thing to mitigate the chill sweeping through his grandfather's living room. The cozy furniture, the warmth of the decor, all seemed covered in a thin layer of ice brought about by Cole's betrayal.

"It's his ambition," Jamison murmured, sitting back and rubbing one hand across his jaw. "His and Susan's. That woman's always pushing Cole for more. I'm not excusing him, mind you. What he did, *he* did. But I am saying he's probably been feeling some pressure."

He looked at Luke. "The way I treated you—favored you over him—probably had a lot to do with it, too."

"No," Luke said. He'd been going over and over this since the moment Fiona had given him the proof of Cole's deception. "You're not taking the blame for this, Pop. What Cole did, he did on his own. If he wanted more responsibility at the company, then he damn well should have earned it. You know as well as I do that he loves the paycheck, he just doesn't want to work.

"He doesn't get to slide on this. You should call the police."

"And tell them what?" Jamison countered with a choked laugh. "That my grandson was gaslighting me? No. This is family, and that's how we'll handle it."

"I agree, Jamie." Loretta's voice was soft but firm.

Luke looked at them both and didn't get it. Cole had hurt the man who'd raised him, loved him. Cole had done awful things, so how could he ever be forgiven for it? Fiona was wrong, he told himself. An apology didn't mean forgiveness, and it certainly didn't mean anyone would forget what had happened.

But this wasn't his call.

"Fine," he said finally. "We'll do it your way. What's the plan?"

"We'll be having a family dinner here tonight," Jamison said, with a glance at his wife to make sure the idea was all right with her. At Loretta's nod, Jamison said, "We'll talk then, and I'll handle Cole."

"I'm sorry it all went to hell. I liked Luke."

"Me, too," Fiona said with a wry smile. She'd relived that last argument, the one they'd had the week before, almost daily. She kept coming up with things she should have said, should have done. Would it have changed anything? Probably not, but he might have at least understood.

For a week, she'd tortured herself while gathering information for his grandfather. Now that job was done, and it was time to admit that whatever she'd had with Luke was just as finished.

"He might come crawling back," Laura mused.

"Luke? Crawl?" Fiona shook her head and laughed.

"That would be something to see. But it would never happen. He's too proud. Too sure of himself and too wrapped up in his boldly black-and-white, right-and-wrong world. He'll never forgive me for lying to him.

"And though I'm sorry it was necessary, I can't completely regret it, because if I hadn't agreed to keep my identity and purpose a secret, I never would have met him in the first place. God. Isn't this a pitiful rant?"

"I've heard worse."

Fiona laughed a little. "That's something, I guess." She reached for a cookie, pulled off a few crumbs and said, "What am I supposed to do now, Laura?"

Her best friend reached across the table, patted her hand and said, "What you always do. Live. Work. Smile."

Fiona's eyes filled with tears. That all sounded impossible at the moment. "It hurts to breathe."

Laura cried with her. "I know, Fee. It's going to for a while. That's why we have wine and cookies."

Briefly, Fiona's lips curved. "And friends."

Then dutifully, she took a bite of her cookie and washed it down with wine.

When Cole and his family arrived, Jamison braced himself. He still didn't want to believe that the boy he'd loved and raised had tried so hard to convince him that he was losing his mind. That was a stab to the heart that was going to take some time to get past.

But he would get past it. This was family and,

despite the current circumstances, Jamison knew Cole was a decent man. Underneath his jealousy of Luke, his blind ambition and desire to take over the company to prove to himself he was just as good as, if not better than Luke, Cole was just a man looking for something he couldn't find.

Jamison hurt for him, but his anger and disappointment were just as vibrant as the pain he felt. He needed to make Cole accept that actions have consequences.

Cole needed to be reminded of what was truly important.

Carrying his son Oliver into the room, Cole was followed by Susan, just a step or two behind them. Cole was wearing khaki slacks, a red polo shirt and loafers while Susan looked as she always did. As if she'd just stepped out of a fashion magazine—cool and beautiful. Oliver, of course, was the shining, smiling boy he was supposed to be. And Jamison meant to keep him that way. Damned if he'd destroy the boy's father to make a point.

Jamison noticed the moment Cole spotted Luke standing at the wet bar in the corner, and Jamison frowned to see the hard resentment on Cole's features. Yes, Jamison told himself. No matter what else, he had to take partial responsibility for this mess. He'd favored Luke and, in doing so, he'd shortchanged Cole. He hadn't meant to. He'd only responded to the boys as their nature—and his— had demanded. But that had been a mistake. Maybe if he'd expected more of Cole, Jamison would have gotten it.

What was the old saying? *People will rise or fall according to your expectations of them.*

In that, he'd let Cole down.

He was about to make up for that.

"Luke," Cole said flatly. "I didn't expect to see you here."

"I'll bet," Luke muttered.

Jamison shot him a quelling look, then said, "Susan, why don't you take Oliver back to Marie? She's made his favorite cookies today and that will give us all a chance to talk."

Their cook loved little Oliver, so Jamison knew the boy would be looked after while the adults had a serious discussion.

"All right." Susan did as asked, and Cole sat down on one of the sofas.

"Want a drink?" Luke asked from the corner.

"Yeah. Scotch."

Loretta took Jamison's hand and gave it a squeeze as he stood up and walked across the room to stand by the fireplace.

Luke delivered Cole's scotch, then took a seat in an armchair near his cousin. Jamison watched them all.

Luke was tense, Loretta was miserable, Cole was clearly uneasy and Susan, when she reentered the room, looked tranquil. That wouldn't last much longer.

Jamison had done plenty of unpleasant things in

his life, but none of them, he thought, compared to this single moment. He loved Cole, but Jamison had been through a nightmare the last few weeks and his grandson was the reason why. That had to be addressed, like it or not.

Cole shot a look at Luke, then turned to his grandfather. "What's going on, Pop?"

"I know what you've been up to, Cole." He kept his gaze fixed on Cole's, so he saw when the man flinched, and it damn near broke Jamison's heart. Yes, he had known it was true. But seeing it on Cole's face just made it so much more painful.

"I don't know what you're talking about."

"Don't lie to him," Luke muttered. "Don't make it even worse."

Cole snapped, "Stay out of this. Why are you even here? You *left*."

"I came back."

"What?" Susan finally spoke and the shock in her voice said volumes.

Jamison knew she'd been counting on her husband taking over the company. Susan wasn't a bad person, but she was a social climber and having her husband as the CEO of a billion-dollar company would be right up her alley.

Cole ignored his wife and turned to Jamison. "You mean, he's back at the company? All is forgiven? Just like that?"

"Just like that," Jamison said, and lifted one hand to Luke, silently telling him to keep quiet. This was for Jamison to do, as much as he wished he didn't have to. "You have anything to say about this, Cole?"

"If you're talking about Luke sliding back into the fold, then yeah. I've got things to say."

"You should be more concerned with yourself than Luke," Jamison told him shortly. "I told you. I know what you've been doing to me."

"Pop—"

The room was so quiet it was as if everyone in it had taken a breath and held it. "I've got evidence, so don't bother denying it."

Eleven

Cole tossed his scotch down his throat, then set the glass on the table in front of him. "I won't. What would be the point?"

"You bastard," Luke muttered.

"That's enough, Luke." Jamison's heart was aching as he looked at his oldest grandson. "Why, Cole? Just so you could take charge?"

"Why shouldn't he?" Susan asked. "He's your grandson, too."

"He is." Jamison nodded. "But as of today, he's not a vice president at the company any longer."

"You can't do that." Susan jumped to her feet and faced Jamison.

"Yes, he can." Cole gave his wife a steely look,

then stood up. He looked directly into Jamison's eyes and said, "I did it. And I swear a part of me thought it was for your sake, too, Pop. Force you to slow down. Retire."

"By making me think I was losing my mind?"

To his credit, Cole flushed and shifted his gaze.

Jamison wasn't nearly finished. "You gave me more than a few hard days. But you made your Gran worry *for* me and that I won't allow."

Cole looked at Loretta and even from across the room, Jamison could read the man's shame. "I'm sorry for this, Gran."

Sadly, she nodded. "I know you are, Cole."

"I don't know that," Jamison said brusquely and waited for Cole to look at him again. "But I'm going to believe that you mean it because I want to. And more importantly, because I need to."

Cole nodded and squared his shoulders. He never again looked at Luke and that, to Jamison's mind, was telling. He was standing on his own and taking it, maybe for the first time in his adult life, and Jamison was glad to see it.

"I am sorry, Pop."

In Jamison's eyes, Cole was still a young boy, devastated at the loss of his parents, coming to live with his grandparents, trying to find his way and failing more often than he succeeded. He'd never been as sure of himself as Luke and, after a time, that had begun to eat at him. Maybe if Jamison had tried to address what Cole was feeling earlier, none of this would have happened.

Loving Cole didn't stop just because he'd been a damn fool. But love didn't mean there'd be no consequences.

"You're not going to be running Barrett's, Cole. You're not going to be trusted with much of anything at the company. Not until you prove yourself to me."

"I understand."

"I don't." Susan nudged her husband, and Cole turned to glare at her.

"Quiet," he said tightly. "Just, be quiet, Susan."

"But it's not right."

"Stop."

Shocked, she closed her mouth, but her eyes were screaming.

When he had quiet again, Jamison said, "You'll be working with Tony in janitorial."

"What?" Susan exclaimed again, and Jamison almost enjoyed watching her stunned expression.

But Cole didn't even flinch, and Jamison gave him full points for that.

"You'll work there until Tony is convinced that you're ready to move up to research. From there, you'll move through the company, earning the respect of every one of our employees."

"I understand." Cole's teeth were gritted and his voice strained, but he didn't argue.

"I hope you do. But, so we're clear on this, Cole," Jamison said, "you'll take the time to learn everything there is to know about this company, to understand every detail *and* the big picture, or you'll be fired."

Stiffly, he nodded.

"This is my offer to you, Cole." Jamison looked only at Cole. It was as if the rest of the room had disappeared. He had to reach his grandson, and this was the only way he knew. "Work your way back up. Earn my trust again. But ultimately, the choice is yours.

"You can do this my way or you can leave the company and strike out on your own."

Cole turned to look at his wife, then slanted a look at Luke, who'd been so still, so quiet, Jamison had almost forgotten he was there.

"I'll stay," Cole said, and lifted his chin. "I'll do whatever I have to do, Pop. And I'll earn your trust again."

"I look forward to that." Nodding, Jamison walked to Cole and stopped right in front of him. "Just so you know, no more yacht club memberships, and your salary won't be a vice president's."

"Oh, now—"

Cole simply ground out, "Susan…"

"I'll see that you can stay in your house," Jamison added, and that mollified Susan a bit. "For Oliver's sake. I don't want my great-grandson uprooted because his father was a damn fool."

"Thanks." Cole swallowed hard and nodded. "It's more than I deserve. And I know that."

Jamison looked into his grandson's eyes for a long minute and was relieved to see what he'd hoped for. Real contrition. Real shame. And a determination that he'd never really seen there before. This might turn out to be the best thing that had ever happened to Cole. Jamison hoped so.

"What you did was bad, Cole," Jamison said, and reached out to clap one hand on the other man's shoulder. "But I love you. Nothing you do can change that."

Hope shone in Cole's eyes before he said, "Thank you for that, too. I'll prove myself, Pop. Even if it takes a decade."

"Good." He squeezed Cole's shoulder and the gratitude in his eyes almost undid Jamison. "Now why don't you take your family home so you and Susan can talk about your new situation."

"I will." He walked to Loretta and bent to kiss her cheek. She patted his hand and gave him an encouraging smile.

When he passed Luke, Cole nodded. Finally, he took Susan's arm and steered her from the room. Jamison dropped onto the nearest couch and sighed, exhausted from the emotional turmoil. "That's not something I ever want to do again."

"I'm just going to the kitchen to see Oliver before they leave." Loretta hurried from the room, leaving the two men alone.

"That's it?" Luke asked. "Start him at the bottom and work his way back up?"

Still tired, Jamison slanted a look at his other grandson. "It's a lesson for him, Luke. The last time he worked janitorial was when he was sixteen. Just like you." Jamison rubbed his eyes trying to ease the headache settled behind them. "For a man like Cole, starting over is the hardest thing for him to face.

"The fact that he accepted it is a good sign. Of course we'll have to see if he actually follows through."

"I think he will," Luke admitted reluctantly.

"Why?"

"He was shocked when you called him on what he'd done. I don't think he ever considered that he'd get caught."

"True."

Frowning to himself, Luke added, "But once he knew you had him, he stood up to it. I'll give him that."

"Sounds like you're easing up on him."

Instantly, Luke shook his head. "Nope. For what he did, there is no forgiveness."

"Oh hell." Jamison pushed out of the chair and walked to the wet bar. He poured himself a scotch and took a sip. "All of us need forgiveness now and then."

"And then it's all good? Slate clean?"

"The slate's never clean," Jamison told him. "Hell, the slate doesn't even start out clean. There's always dust or something on it. And when we wipe away the bad stuff, there's a shadow, an echo of what's been there before. But that's all there is. Just a shadow. And we're free to write on the slate again—good or bad."

Luke stared into his glass and the expression on his face told Jamison he was thinking about his own "slate." Jamison had a feeling he knew what Luke was thinking about and being a man who always had an opinion and didn't mind sharing it, Jamison started talking again.

"Fiona's a miracle worker, I swear."

Luke's gaze shot to his. "I suppose. She came through this time, anyway."

"Came through with you, too," Jamison said.

"By lying? Sure." Luke took a sip of his scotch and sat there glowering like a gargoyle.

"Lies are slippery things," Jamison mused as if to himself. "I tell them and say your Gran looks good in that ugly blue dress she loves, and she kisses me. Cole tells them, and it destroyed what he most wanted. Fiona tells them, and you're back with the company where you belong."

Luke just stared at him. "You're not exactly subtle. You know that, right?"

Jamison chuckled. "Wasn't trying to be. What Fiona did, she did because I hired her. She couldn't exactly show up and tell you why she was there, could she?"

"She could have told me later. After—"

"Maybe she was afraid you'd take it badly," Jamison said wryly.

"Maybe," Luke allowed, still staring into his scotch as if searching for answers in that amber liquid. After a long minute or two, he said, almost to himself, "And maybe there's no forgiveness for what I said to her once I knew the truth."

"Both of my grandsons...damn fools. There's only one way to find out if she'll forgive you." Luke looked at him and Jamison blurted out impatiently, "For God's sake, boy, go and get her. Convince her to take a shot on you."

A brief smile curved Luke's mouth. "And start over with a clean slate?"

"Write a new story."

The next day, Fiona realized she was doing just what Laura had advised.

She lived. She worked.

She wasn't smiling yet, but she'd get there. Eventually.

"And you're helping, aren't you, George?" Fiona bent down to frame the giant dog's face. A Bernese mountain dog, George weighed a hundred and twenty pounds and was living under the delusion that he was a lap dog.

George lifted one huge paw and laid it on her forearm. Fiona staggered a little but found a small smile just for him. Dog sitting was one of the jobs she most loved doing. Having George in her house for the next week while his family was at Disney World would give her comfort and company.

"You're such a good boy," she said, and gave his big head another brisk rub. "You want to go for a walk?"

George barked and wiggled all over. Thankfully, Fiona had already taken all the breakables off low tables so his swishing tail couldn't do much damage.

"I'll take that as a yes," she said and picked up the leash. Hooking it to his collar, she grabbed a couple of poop bags, just in case, and opened the front door.

"Hello, Fiona."

Her heart stopped. Actually stopped.

When she took a sudden deep breath, it started again and almost made her dizzy. The one person in the world she never would have expected to find on her porch was standing there staring at her.

"Luke?"

As if sensing her distress, George stepped in front of her, looked up at Luke and growled from deep in his throat.

Luke took a step back. "Whoa. You have a pony now?"

A short, sharp laugh shot from her throat. "This is George. I'm dog sitting for a neighbor." Looking down at the big dog, she ran one hand over his thick neck and smooth, beautiful fur. "He's very protective. It's okay, George. Luke is a...*friend.*"

The dog calmed down, but Luke said, "Am I? A friend?"

She shrugged, not knowing what to make of this. "He knows that word, so he'll calm down."

"You didn't answer the question, Fiona."

"I don't know the answer, Luke." She didn't know anything. Obviously. She hadn't expected to ever see Luke again, yet here he was. His hair was a little longer now, and his summer-blue eyes were locked on her. He wore one of his perfect suits and managed somehow to look both businesslike and dangerously attractive.

She was trying to get over him. To let go of him and everything that might have been. Having him show up at her house wasn't exactly helping.

"He needs to take a walk," she said, stepping outside with George and forcing Luke to step back farther. She closed her door and stopped again when Luke stood in front of her.

"Can I go with you?"

She wanted to shout *yes!* Because she'd missed him so much. Missed talking to him, looking at him, kissing him, laughing with him, kissing him, curling up next to him, their naked bodies still warm from the sex that haunted her with detailed, torturous memories.

Apparently, Luke saw her indecision, because he said, "I need to talk to you, Fiona."

That decided her. "What's left to say, Luke?"

Sunlight drifted through the branches of the trees and a soft, cold wind slid past them.

"A lot, I think. Will you listen?"

She looked into his eyes and tried to decide why he was there. What else he might want to say to her?

And finally, Fiona realized that the only way to get through this was to get it over with.

"Walk and talk," she said, and let George pull her down the walkway to the sidewalk out front.

George was in seventh heaven, sniffing at every tree, every blade of grass. He turned his face into the wind, shook his head and kept going. Thankfully, he had been well trained for the leash because if she'd had to hold him back, Fiona never would have been able to.

"Pop settled the situation with Cole," Luke said, and she glanced at him.

"I'm glad."

"He didn't fire him." Luke frowned a bit at that. "I thought he should have, but Pop wouldn't hear anything about it."

She shrugged. "He's family." And Fiona, who had never had a family of her own, understood the importance of that relationship. Knew what a gift it was and how hard it would be to deny.

"Yeah. He's been seriously demoted, though. He has to work his way through every department in the company, earning respect along the way, before he'll be allowed back in completely."

"He'll do it," Fiona said firmly.

"You're so sure?"

"I am. He knows now what he almost lost. He'll fight to get it all back." That's what she would do.

"Can he?" Luke asked.

She looked up at him when George stopped to mark a tree.

"Of course. Your grandfather loves him. Love doesn't just stop one day because things get hard or ugly."

"I'm glad to hear you say that."

Luke took her arm and turned her to face him. God, he'd missed her. Just being beside her. Looking into her warm chocolate eyes. The only thing missing was her smile and he knew that *he* was the reason behind that. It killed him now to remember what he'd said to her. How he'd treated her.

And he knew how Cole must have felt standing before their grandfather. Unsure of whether he'd be forgiven—or even if he deserved forgiveness.

Suspicion flashed in her eyes. "Why?"

"Because I need you to forgive me, Fiona. I said some really crappy things to you." Which didn't even start to cover it. "I'm sorry for it. Maybe I was looking at things like you said, black and white, right and wrong, and I forgot—or didn't want to know that there are shades of gray, too. My view was so narrow I couldn't see what I was missing. I looked at my job, my family, my company in a single vision and didn't notice that other things were there, too.

"And I saw your lies and didn't look for more. I should have. You're the one who opened me up, Fiona. Taught me to look beyond the obvious and I should have done that with you, too. I want you to know I didn't mean a word of what I said before. I was just—"

"Furious? Hurt?"

"Both," he admitted.

"I understand that. So yes. I forgive you."

"Thank you." He smiled. "And now I can tell you that the main reason I came here today was to hire you for another job. I've lost something important."

"Oh."

Disappointment shone in her eyes, and Luke felt like an ass. At the same time, a flicker of hope rose up in his chest.

After a second or two, she asked, "What did you lose?"

"My heart." Luke watched her reaction and saw confusion there now, which was way better than disappointment. "My heart's been lost since the moment I met you."

Her eyes widened and her breathing quickened. All good signs. Then she asked, "Are you sure you had one to begin with?"

One corner of his mouth lifted briefly. "A fair question. And yes, I'm sure. It was a hard ball of ice in my chest and when I lost it, warmth came back." He kept his gaze locked on hers, searching for what he wanted, *needed* to see. "I didn't even recognize it for the gift it was," he admitted. "I didn't appreciate that warmth until it was gone, and the ice was back."

"Luke…"

He cut her off. "I'm not saying it'll be easy to find

my heart. Might take years. Might take forever. Are you willing to take on a long-term job like that?"

George tugged on the leash, clearly impatient with the humans interfering with his walk. Fiona laughed and the sound swept through Luke like a warm breeze. He'd missed it. He'd missed so much.

"I don't know, Luke," she said, shaking her head. "I want to believe you, I really do."

"Then do it." He took the leash from her hand, looked at George and said firmly, *"Sit."*

Once the dog complied, he turned back to her. "I was an ass, Fiona."

"No argument."

He snorted. "I deserve that. I was wrong. If it weren't for the lies you told for my grandfather, I never would have met you and—" He shook his head. "I can't even imagine not knowing you. Not loving you."

She sucked in a gulp of air. "Love?"

"Yeah," he said, rubbing the backs of his fingers against her cheek. "Surprised me, too. And maybe that's why I was acting like such a jackass. I'd never been in love before, so I didn't appreciate it. Didn't really recognize it. But I do now.

"I love you, Fiona. I want you. I need you. But mostly, I can't even picture living my life without you."

Fiona sighed and he hoped it was with happiness. But he kept talking because he couldn't take the chance of losing her now.

"I'm asking you to marry me, Fiona."

"Oh my God." She staggered back a step, and he tightened his grip on her. "I can't believe this."

"Believe it. Believe me," he urged. "I want to marry you. I want us to have that family you used to dream of having. Kids, Fiona."

She inhaled sharply, her heart clenching as he offered her…everything.

"I want us to build something amazing together. And I really hope you want all of that, too."

Lifting one hand to cover her mouth, her gaze was locked with his and he saw what he'd hoped to see in those dark brown depths. Love. Acceptance. Forgiveness.

And Luke took his first easy breath in more than a week.

She reached up and cupped his cheek in her palm, and the heat of her touch slid through him like a blessing, easing away the last of the chill that had been with him since he'd sent her away.

"I want all of that, too, Luke. I do love you. So much."

He let out a breath he hadn't realized he'd been holding. "Thank God."

"I want you, too. I love you, Luke. Maybe I have right from that first day. And I'd love to build a family with you." Tears glimmered in her eyes, making them shine with hope and a promise for the future. *Their* future.

The big dog wandered over, leaned against Luke's

leg and nearly toppled him. When he would have snapped at the beast, George looked up at him with adoration. Luke sighed and petted him before digging into his pants pocket for a blue velvet ring box.

Fiona saw it and gasped.

"I don't understand the shock," he said, smiling. "I proposed, you accepted. A ring is traditional."

She laughed. "I know, it's just…this is all so not what I expected to happen today."

Luke opened the box to show her the ring he'd chosen for her. A huge dark emerald surrounded by diamonds winked in the afternoon sun.

She looked up at him. "It's beautiful."

He took the ring from its perch and slid it onto her finger. "When I saw it, it made me think of that dark green shirt you were wearing the day we met. The day you fell into my lap and completely changed my world."

A lone tear escaped her eye to roll down her cheek. He caught it with a fingertip and kissed it away.

"This is the most romantic thing that's ever happened to me," she said, lifting her gaze from the ring to the man who'd given it to her.

"Even with George here?"

At the sound of his name, George barked and looked from one to the other of them, a smile on his face as if he were in on the secret.

"Especially with George here," she said, laughing. "Which reminds me, I always wanted a dog."

"Deal," he said, then stroked the big dog's head. "Maybe George has a cousin who needs a home."

If not, Luke would find one. A dog like George. To always remind him of this day. This moment. When Fiona loved him.

"You're offering me everything I ever dreamed of," Fiona said softly. "Someone to love and be loved by. Someone to make a family with. Someone who will always be there, standing beside me."

"All of that and more, Fiona." He swore it to her and to himself.

She went to him and hooked her arms around his neck, holding on tightly as if afraid he might slip away. But she didn't have to worry, Luke told himself as he held her just as close. He'd never lose her again.

He pulled his head back then and grinned at her. "Oh, there's something else, too. Jamison wants to see you."

"About what?"

"Something about keeping an eye on Cole for a while to make sure it's all working out with him."

"Do you think it will?" she asked, still holding on to him, staring into his eyes.

"I know it will," Luke said. "He got a second chance. Pop loved him enough to forgive him. To start over. Cole won't blow that chance."

Still looking up at him, Fiona asked, "And we've forgiven each other, so the same thing holds true?"

"We've got a clean slate, Fiona," Luke said. "No

echoes, no shadows. Just a brand-new story we get to write. Together."

She grinned. "What does that mean?"

It meant, he thought, that shades of gray were beautiful.

"I'll tell you later," he promised. Then he kissed her and his world came right again. Everything was good. Everything was...perfect.

* * * * *

Look for more sexy, emotional romances from USA TODAY bestselling author Maureen Child!

Tempt Me in Vegas
Bombshell for the Boss
Red Hot Rancher